CAIRO JIM

AND THE LAGOON OF
TIDAL MAGNIFICENCE

A Sumatran Tale of Splendour

GEOFFREY McSKIMMING

WALKER
BOOKS

▲▲▲▲▲ CONTENTS ▲▲▲▲▲

"In the jungle, footsteps are obliterated by every shower."

–F.M. Schnitger,
Forgotten Kingdoms of Sumatra (1938)

Part One:

MANY SECRETS
AT HAND

A MOVEABLE BEAST

"AND, LADIES, in conclusion, please believe me when I tell you that your fingers will be enveloped in a total rhapsody of comfort!"

The large, fleshy man held his arms wide and surveyed his audience through his horn-rimmed spectacles. A trickle of sweat emerged from beneath his third chin (he had, at last count, six chins at the base of his wide, chubby face) and dribbled down to his collar.

His audience – all eight members of the Turkish Women's Olympic Championship Tent Erection Team – stared at him dubiously.

Each of the women was astonishingly hefty.

Each had an uncountable number of rock-solid muscles bulging underneath her lilac-coloured tracksuit.

Each of the women looked far from impressed.

"Yes, ladies," the man continued in a voice less bold than before, "the totally new, never-before-available Glamourdust Tent-pegging Gloves with the reinforced, rubberised thumb guard and gentle latex finger paddings will be the answer to *all* your dreams!"

The man stood before them, his arms still outstretched. Then, as the silence became thick and uncomfortable, he lowered his arms and took a big,

peach-coloured, osnaburg handkerchief from the pocket of his plus-fours trousers. He dabbed the handkerchief heavily at his chins.

"Er, ladies," he ventured, "perhaps I was speaking a tad too quickly for you all to comprehend the importance of what I was saying. Let me take it a little slower…"

"We understood you, mister!"

The loud, throaty voice broke the silence like a fog horn blares through a misty night.

"We understood," repeated Fatimé Breeches, the Captain of the Turkish Women's Olympic Championship Tent Erection Team. She stood, raising her tall, wide body from the bench on which she had been sitting, and hitched up her tracksuit pants. "Didn't we, girls?"

The other seven women nodded their massive heads and rumbled in agreement.

"It is just that we are not trusting of you," Fatimé Breeches said.

The man's eyes widened behind his spectacles. "Not trusting of *me*, Preston Glamourdust? How can this be?"

"We've never heard of you." Fatimé frowned. "Or your company."

Preston Glamourdust squinted at her and thought quickly. He knew that there might be some resistance to his plan: these women were far from happy, having recently lost the Championship Tent Erection Gold Medal at the last Olympic Games. He had heard that since their disastrous and humiliating defeat, they had sacked their coach and were now trusting no one.

"The reason you have not heard of me, ladies, is because my company is new to your country. This is the first month that I have opened my business in Turkey. But, rest assured, the Glamourdust Glove and Gusset Company is remarkably famous throughout fourteen European and six African countries. Not to mention the east coast of Tasmania."

The women looked harshly at him.

"'We cover the extremities in most of the *world's* extremities!', as one of our slogans goes."

He paused, letting them take in the information.

"I am, so to speak, a fresh player on the field here in Turkey."

"Well," said Fatimé Breeches, frowning again, "fresh player or not, why should we look at your tent-pegging gloves?"

"Yes," boomed the tent-pole-securing member of the Team, a towering, thickly padded woman named Kaynarca. "What's so special about yours?"

"Well," said Preston Glamourdust, his lips spreading into a wide smile under his neatly trimmed beard (like two fat slugs sliding through a hairy garden), "apart from the features I have already told you about, there is something very special about our new Glamourdust Tent-pegging Gloves which sets them apart from all other brands. Something that, had you been equipped with it at the recent Olympic Games, would have assured your Team absolute victory over the Venezuelan Women's Olympic Championship Tent Erection Team!"

The women of the Turkish Women's Olympic Championship Tent Erection Team leant forward on their benches. Fatimé Breeches folded her arms and waited, her brows lowering.

"Let me show you a diagram," said Preston Glamourdust.

He turned around and bent over to rummage in a suitcase on the floor behind him. Those in the front row visibly shuddered at the sight of his capacious bottom stretching the fabric of his Crimplene plus-fours trousers. (It looked like a couple of watermelons squeezed into a badly made sock.)

"Ah! Here it is." He straightened, turned, and displayed a large diagram of a single glove. "To be strictly accurate, ladies, this is a tent-pegging *gauntlet*."

Several of the women raised their muscular eyebrows.

"But we at Glamourdust have modified the design so that it maintains an air of femininity."

"We don't care about *that*," said Fatimé. "Tell us about this very special feature!"

"Yes," shouted one of the tent-rope tighteners, a solid, no-nonsense woman named Osmana. "How could it have helped us win at the Olympics?"

Preston Glamourdust pursed his lips. Never had he encountered such a tough group as this. He took a deep breath and, with his chubby index finger, pointed to an area on the diagram that ran between the ring-finger socket and the thumb socket.

"Behold, ladies, the thing that makes our tent-pegging gloves unique from other tent-pegging gloves. The revolutionised, non-slip, cleft-caressing *fourchettes*!"

"The fourchettes?" repeated a few of the women.

"Arrr, yes, the areas of the glove that consist of those forked strips of material which link the front and back parts of the finger sections. The Glamourdust fourchettes are second to none!"

Fatimé turned to the other women. "That's the part that let us down at the Games! The wretched fourchettes!"

One of the bulky women growled quietly at the bitter memory.

"I was watching the event on the television," said Mr Glamourdust solemnly, "and I said to myself, 'Preston, that is a woman betrayed by her fourchettes!'"

The largest woman in the group stood, planting her enormous feet heavily on the wooden floor. She was taller and wider and broader than any of the other two women in the room put together. "Those rotten gloves we had that day cost us the gold medals!" she seethed. "All because they split around the finger bits when I was hammering in the final tent pegs!"

Fatimé reached up and put her hand firmly on the woman's shoulder. "There, there. We can't cry over spilt milk for ever, Dënise."

Dënise was turning red as her rage gathered around and inside her like a surging burst of cloud. "It was because of the weak stitching, and the roughness of the material in the ... what did you call them, man?"

"The fourchettes," answered Preston Glamourdust.

"Yes, it was because of the lousy fourchettes that I let the Team down. The sides of my fingers were chafing from those rough gloves, and the handle of my tent-pegging mallet was rubbing against them ... rubbing, rubbing, rubbing ... it completely wore the fourchettes' stitching away. I only had three whacks on that final peg to go. THREE STRONG WHACKS!" A fat tear formed in her eye. "If only the hammer hadn't flown out of my glove when the fourchettes split ... if only that shot-putter from Rarotonga hadn't been doing up his shoelaces at that very moment."

"There, there, Dënise, they managed to get the hammer out again."

Dënise sniffed loudly and sat heavily down.

Fatimé turned back to Preston Glamourdust. "These fourchettes you speak of, Mr Glamourdust. Can you guarantee that they are stronger than any others?"

"Absolutely, madam."

"And they will not rub against Dënise's fingers?"

"I give you my word. They have been tested on specially selected gorillas, trained for this very purpose."

Fatimé raised her thick eyebrows.

"The gorillas liked them so much, in fact, that we couldn't get them to give the gloves back to us. There is now a group of the creatures in the highlands of Rwanda who are very well decked out from their wrists down."

"A diagram is no good," blurted Kaynarca. "Why don't you show us the real thing?"

"Yes!" hollered Osmana. "Let us make up our minds with our hands!"

The other members of the Team growled in agreement.

Dënise leapt up again and grabbed Preston Glamourdust by the front of his collar, lifting him until he had to stand on the tips of his chubby toes. "I could whack a couple of dozen tent pegs into the concrete outside to test out these fourchettes well and proper," she said, eyeballing him impatiently.

"What a splendid idea," squeaked Preston Glamourdust, his eyes bulging and his forehead awash with sweat. He dropped the diagram back into his suitcase and tried to wriggle from her vice-like grip. "I would be happy to show you all a pair of these wonderful new gloves … *gleeerrgh*!"

"Good," said Fatimé.

"Good," grunted Dënise, letting go of his collar.

He gulped several times and took a very deep breath. When he was breathing normally again, and the colour had returned to his bearded cheeks, he smiled and spoke as if nothing had happened. "If you would all be so kind as to step outside with me, to the Glamourdust pantechnicon, which is parked in the alley at the rear of this building, I will show you these delights for the digits."

"In a *truck*?" asked Fatimé, her throaty voice even more throaty than usual.

"Our mobile display vehicle, madam." He closed his suitcase and picked it up. "We have such a wide range of gloves and gussets, it is much more sensible to travel around with them all in the one, easy-to-view location. It saves my company much time and expense. Now, if you will all follow me, I'm sure your fingers are just *itching* to be thrust into the delights of my merchandise."

He strode confidently to the door, his huge stomach wobbling beneath his paisley-swirled shirt and his emerald-green waistcoat. "After you," he smiled, holding the door open for Fatimé and her Team.

"Come, girls," she said. "Let's see if these gloves are as good as the words pouring out from those lips of his."

"They'd better be," whispered Dënise in such a threatening tone that the man's beard bristled.

Outside, in the damp, narrow alley behind their headquarters, the Turkish Women's Olympic Championship Tent Erection Team stopped at the rear of the large pantechnicon.

Stuck across the van's side was a big, painted advertisement. On it there was a smiling woman with dazzling blonde hair and more teeth than would have been possible in anyone's mouth who *wasn't* painted on the side of a large pantechnicon. She was wearing a pair of bright blue gloves and cupping her face so that she looked as if she had two baby blue octopuses sticking out from the sides of her cheeks.

Underneath the glove-cheeked woman was the brightly painted slogan:

Just *Everybody* Loves
Glamourdust Gloves!

The back doors to the pantechnicon were open, and Preston Glamourdust ushered the women towards them. "Go on, ladies, please step inside."

"Me first!" Dënise elbowed several of her Team mates out of the way and pushed herself into the van.

"You will find the Tent-pegging Gloves on the wall display to the right of the van." Mr Glamourdust watched as the Team boarded his vehicle. "Go all the way in. Right up to the front, that's the way."

"It's a bit dark in there," complained Fatimé Breeches.

"Never mind, madam, I shall turn on the lights when you are all inside … there, up the step, that's the way." He narrowed his eyes and watched as Fatimé entered the pantechnicon. She was the last to board.

The fat man stepped back and raised his fingers to his mouth. With a great blow, he whistled piercingly into the alley.

"Wait a momentum," came one of the women's voices from inside the van. "There are no—"

A smudge of dark feathers swooped through the alley, knocking against one of the rear doors. The door slammed shut with a crash. Then the smudge knocked against the other door and it, too, slammed shut.

A set of pudgy fingers quickly locked the doors.

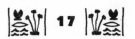

The women thumped the insides of the van, loudly and angrily.

The horn-rimmed spectacles were flung into a greasy puddle.

The man and the smudge of feathers ripped the painted sign from the side of the van. Both man and smudge hurried into the driver's compartment at the front and, with a loud revving of the engine, the pantechnicon sped out of the alley and off into the evening gloom of Istanbul.

WITH HOLIDAY EYES

CAIRO JIM, THE WELL-KNOWN archaeologist and little-known poet, packed the last of his essential belongings into his knapsack and came out of his much-patched tent into the bold Egyptian sunshine.

He quickly donned his special desert sun-spectacles as the brightness rushed at him. Even though he had spent many years based here near the Valley of the Kings, the glare of the sun off the desert dunes still took him by surprise.

He put on his pith helmet, hitched his knapsack across a shoulder, and went to see how his friend, the learned and brave macaw, Doris, was getting on with her packing.

"Rark!" screeched the yellow-and-blue-feathered bird when she saw him. She was sitting on the collapsible writing table, surrounded by all sorts of paraphernalia. "Do you have room in your knapsack for these few things?"

"I'm sure I do." Jim smiled at her. "I'm taking my biggest knapsack this time, so there'll be plenty of – wait a moment, Doris!"

Doris waited for a moment. Then she said, "What's wrong, Jim?"

He tilted his pith helmet back and shook his head. "Do you really want to take *all* of this?"

"Just a few necessary little things," she squawked. "You said to bring 'just a few necessary little things'. I've done what you said."

He looked across the array of bits and pieces she had gathered and organised on the table. "My dear, I don't mind you taking your valuable first edition of the plays of William Shakespeare along with you—"

"Glad to hear it."

"And I don't mind you bringing your pack of cards and your favourite cup—"

"Brenda and I like an evening game of canasta now and then," she said, and blinked. "And you know how fussy I am about drinking from strange vessels, like coconut husks and curled-up leaves."

"Yes, Doris, that's fine. But I wouldn't call some of these other things 'necessary'. Would you?"

"I most certainly would," she said in a tone of bird-like indignation.

"Well," Jim said patiently, "tell me: what's so necessary about this framed photograph of you and me outside the Great Sphinx?"

"It reminds me of the great archaeological discovery we made up there.★ And it reminds me of you."

★ See *Cairo Jim and the Secret Sepulchre of the Sphinx – A Tale of Incalculable Inversion*

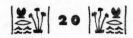 20

Cairo Jim smiled. "But, my dear, I'll be with you while we're away."

"Yes," she said, raising her beak, "but not in black-and-white. You'll be there in the flesh, in full colour. Sometimes I like to think of you in black-and-white... I don't know why, it must be a bird thing. So if I take this photo along, I'm able to indulge my desires. I only have to look at it, and there you are. Rerark."

"All right, Doris, you win." He slipped the framed photo, the Shakespeare folio, her cards and favourite cup into his knapsack. "But what about *these*?" He held up two tiny knitted tubes. "What're these? Coats for pencils?"

"No, of course not." She blinked at him again, and explained patiently. "They're leg warmers. For me. In case it gets cold."

"Leg warmers?"

"Rark."

"But we're off to Sumatra! Into the jungles! It'll be hot there, not cold."

"The plane might be overly air-conditioned."

"Then you can snuggle into one of my spare socks," he said, putting her leg warmers back on the table. "And what do you want with this half-eaten mango?"

"I thought it'd be a shame to let it go to waste."

"A shame it has to be." He placed that back on the table as well, and picked up another object. "And *this*?"

She opened and closed her huge wings. "I thought we might have time for a round or two."

"But you don't even *play* golf!" He put the golf club back. "And we haven't got room for your potted coquilla-nut palm tree, either."

"But it's only small!"

"Or for your framed collection of knot-language examples from ancient civilisations of South America."

"Rerk."

"Or your antique rubber-band collection."

She flexed herself up and down, and the feathers at the edge of her beak crinkled.

"And what's *this*?"

"It's ornamental!"

"An ornamental *lump of rock*?"

"Look carefully. It's not just *any* old lump of rock. If you hold it at the right angle, it looks just like the Prime Minister of Sweden!"

"I'm sorry, my dear." The Prime Minister of Sweden lookalike rock went back on the table.

"Can I have these tins of imported Malawian snails? Please, please, please? You know they're my favourite food of all time…"

"Of course you can, Doris."

"Yippee. Rark!"

"But not thirty-six of them. No, we'll pack a *dozen* tins and that's it. They'll have to go in Brenda's saddle-bags. I'm sure we'll find something similar in Sumatra for you, and anyway, we don't want Brenda's saddlebags bulging again, do we?"

"No," answered the macaw. "Last time she bulged,

that doctor fellow on the train thought she had some rare skin disease."

"Epidemic Camelidae parotitis."

"He wanted to put her into quarantine for twelve months. Poor Brenda!"

At the sound of her name, Brenda the Wonder Camel, the third member of Cairo Jim's renowned archaeological team, came lumbering to them with her saddlebags dangling by a strap from her mouth. She halted by her friends and fluttered her long, thick eyelashes to try to cool her eyelids.

"Brenda, my lovely." Jim took the saddlebags from her and stroked her snout. "Thanks for these. We'll just put our last few things inside them and then we can be off."

Brenda had a thought: *A holiday at last!* And, in true Wonder Camel style, the thought travelled out of her brain and into the open air, where it was soon picked up.

"A holiday at last," Doris crowed as Jim put the tins of snails into the saddlebags (next to Brenda's latest Melodious Tex western adventure novel, *Melodious Tex and the Referendum of Rancid Ravine*).

"Mm-hm," he mm-hmed, as he checked the underside of Brenda's macramé saddle.

"So what time does our plane leave?" asked Doris.

Jim looked at the Cutterscrog Old Timers Archaeological Timepiece on his wrist. "Oh, I'd say in about ten minutes or so."

"*Preeeraaaark!* We'd better be getting to the airport. We don't want to miss it. I don't want to have to fly all the way to Sumatra using my wings."

"Settle down, Doris. We're not going to miss our plane."

"No?" she squawked dubiously.

"Quaaaooo?" Brenda snorted curiously.

"No way. As a matter of fact, here it comes now."

"Eh?"

"Quaaooo?"

"Up there. From the north."

They looked into the northern sky, shielding their eyes from the glare.

"I don't see anything," Doris muttered.

"Look carefully," said Jim. "See? That tiny, almost minuscule black dot?"

Brenda was the next to see it, and she let out a snort of discovery.

Far, far away, the tiny dot was growing bigger and bigger against the great expanse of blue sky. As it got closer, it changed its shape, slowly and gradually, until two small wing-like shapes stuck out from its sides.

"Rark. It's a plane, all right."

"A silver one," Brenda thought.

"A silver one," added Doris.

"Joss's Lockheed Vega," Jim told them.

Doris opened her wings, fluttered into the air, and came to land on his shoulder. "Joss's? You mean Jocelyn Osgood's?"

"I do," Jim replied happily.

"Since when is *she* going to be our pilot?"

Brenda watched as the plane now took on a most recognisable outline.

"Since last week," Jim said. "Valkyrian Airways were going to get rid of the plane – it was old, but still in good condition – and Joss decided to buy it from them. With the staff discount they gave her, it didn't cost her much at all."

Doris shuddered as she heard the noise of the engine. *I don't need any staff discounts to enable* me *to fly* she thought to herself.

"And," continued Jim, "when I told her we were wanting to go to Sumatra for a short holiday break, she decided to take some of her own vacation time from Valkyrian – she had a lot owing, on account of all the extra Flight Attending she's been doing for the company – and come with us. She thought if she flew us there, we'd all save money, and kill two birds with the one stone."

"*Screeeeeeeeeeeerraaaaaaaarrkkkkkkk!*"

Jim jumped at Doris's sudden outburst. "I'm so sorry, my dear. I forgot what an offensive expression that is to you."

"Apology accepted," she mumbled.

"*Look,*" thought Brenda. "*She's coming in to land on that flat bit of desert near the entrance to the Valley of the Hairdressers!*"

"Look," observed Jim. "She's coming in to land on that flat bit of desert near the entrance to the Valley of the Hairdressers!"

The plane circled overhead and, as it dipped its starboard wing, they caught sight of Jocelyn in the cockpit, with her tangly auburn curls shining brightly in the sunshine.

"Come on," said the archaeologist-poet. "Let's tidy up and go to meet her."

"She'd better not try to tie any of those stupid silk ribbons on my feathers again," Doris muttered beneath her breath.

Fifteen minutes later, the aeroplane was trundling across the stretch of hard, compacted sand close to the roadway that led into the Valley of the Hairdressers. The silver propellers glinted as they slowed to a gradual halt, deflecting the sunlight across the dunes and onto Jim's tent in a crazy, haphazard kaleidoscope of brilliance.

Over the purr of the engine, Jim murmured to himself, "Welcome back, Jocelyn Osgood."

The plane turned and stopped. After ten seconds, the side door was flung open and a small set of stairs popped out, connecting the aircraft to the ground. Down these stairs emerged Jocelyn Osgood, Valkyrian Airways' most experienced Senior Flight Attendant, her powder-blue jodhpurs swishing and her curls ruffling in the faint desert breeze.

She stood on the sand for a few seconds, scanning the scene before her. Then she saw Jim, Doris and Brenda. She tore off her flying goggles and hurried across the sand.

"Jim! Great to see you again!"

Jim held out his hand, his ears feeling a strange sort

of happiness (if ears can feel happiness) at the warm and confident sound of her voice. "Great to see you too, Joss."

She bypassed his hand and, leaning forward, gave him a tiny kiss on his cheek (Doris, perched on Jim's shoulder, moved quickly out of the way, thinking that the kiss was meant for *her*). The archaeologist-poet blushed and smiled.

"Doris, you beautiful bird! Hello!" Jocelyn gently tousled Doris's crest.

"Rerark!" Doris jerked her head out of the way, but in a movement that would not upset Jocelyn's feelings. "Greetings, Jocelyn Osgood. It seems we're holidaying together."

Jocelyn smiled widely, her pearly white teeth shining. "We most certainly are. Brenda! You're looking fine, hale and hearty, you gorgeous Wonder Camel."

Brenda snorted and fluttered her luxuriant eyelashes as Jocelyn ran her fingers down her snout (Brenda's, not Jocelyn's).

"Good flight down from Cairo?" asked Jim.

"Fair," Jocelyn replied. "Bit of a sandstorm above the Bahariyya Oasis, but otherwise, all clear."

Doris flexed herself up and down. "C'mon, then. We don't want to stand around in this blazing sunshine all day chit-chatting. Not unless we all want sunstroke."

"No," said Jocelyn. "One tends to loop the loop without realising it if one tries to fly with sunstroke. The passengers don't like that, and neither does

Valkyrian – it means enormous dry-cleaning bills afterwards. Not that we have to worry about Valkyrian Airways on *this* trip."

"Absolutely not," said Jim.

Jocelyn bit her lip for a second. "There was a woman once who drowned on a flight – with another airline, of course – when the pilot looped the loop. Very tragic."

"Rerark! Drowned on an aeroplane?"

"Yes, she was in the lavatory at the time, and … oh, it's not really a tale worth telling." She looked at Jim's knapsack and Brenda's saddlebags. "All packed, then?"

"All packed," said Jim.

"Well, let's get up into that stratosphere." Jocelyn fetched one of Brenda's saddlebags, and Jim the other.

Doris flew onto Brenda's fore hump and, by rustling her wings against Brenda's ears, feathered her towards the plane.

Jocelyn lowered her voice to a whisper, so only Jim could hear. "I had the rear four seats taken out, to make plenty of room for Brenda."

Cairo Jim smiled. "Very good of you, Joss. She'll be as comfortable as us."

"And why shouldn't she be? She's every bit as important."

Doris stood tip-claw on Brenda's fore hump and gazed at the plane. Even though she was normally not very fond of planes – she regarded them as *artificial* fliers and pretenders of the air – there was something special about this aircraft. After all, Jocelyn had never had one that she could truly call her own before.

"Can we go in, Jocelyn Osgood?" squawked the macaw excitedly.

"Of course."

Doris flew off Brenda and into the plane.

"Go on, Brenda, up near the back. There's a special place for you."

"Quaaaoo!"

Brenda stood at the foot of the steps and peered into the interior. Carefully she took a big sniff of the air in there. Yes, she thought, there is safety in this place. Safety, and the faint smell of aviation fuel intermingled with Jocelyn Osgood's perfume, which was like freesias and gardenias mixed together.

And what was that on the floor in the rear, in the space where clearly some seats had been removed?

"I bought that carpet at the bazaar in Cairo," said Jocelyn. "It had your name written all over it, Brenda."

"Rark!" Doris perched on the back of the co-pilot's seat. "Who on earth would have woven a carpet with "Brenda" written all over it?"

"Just a figure of speech, my dear," Jim told her.

"Oh." She blinked. "I knew that." She rolled her small eyes and pondered the strange figures of speech that humans used.

Carefully Brenda went up the four steps, and into the plane. She approached the Brenda carpet and slowly lowered herself onto it, folding her legs beneath her.

"Quaooooo," she snorted happily, rolling her large head in a circle.

"After you, Joss." Jim gestured for her to board. With a wink she entered and ducked into the cockpit.

"Come up here, Jim, next to me. You've got the co-pilot's seat."

"But I know nothing about—"

"It doesn't matter, this thing practically flies itself. Oh, I've been looking forward to this trip for such a long time – for the past week I've been seeing almost every-thing through holiday eyes."

"Holiday eyes?" said Doris, fluttering to nestle in the space in the cockpit between Jocelyn and Jim.

"Mm-hm," Jocelyn mm-hmed, putting on her flying goggles again. "You know, when you're excited about going away. *Really* excited. Well, everything that you see – each everyday object – looks different. Almost golden, and without the usual ordinariness to it. Somehow more special. I don't know how, or why, but everything does. I've always put it down to having 'holiday eyes'."

"Coo," cooed Doris.

"Holiday eyes," Jim said quietly as Jocelyn began to check all the instruments on the control panel. The idea started swirling around in his mind, taking on a shape and form and shooting into his poetry cells. In the next instant, without even realising it, he was reciting:

"We're seeing things through holiday eyes
where what is normal is full of surprise,
and who knows what, in jungle green

awaits us – how will it be seen
if we've all got vacation sight –
will night be day, and day be night?"

"*Screerraaarrk!*" screeched Doris, and everybody jumped. She had the highest opinion of Jim's talent as an *archaeologist*, but his reputation as a poet was not something she was likely to crow about, except to shut him up.

"Quaaaaooo," snorted Brenda in the back. She had always had a soft spot for Jim's poetic tendencies.

"Right," said Jocelyn, who had never made her feelings about his poetry clear. "We're all ready."

"Sumatra here we come!" Doris announced.

Jocelyn flicked a switch and the entrance steps were automatically raised. With a soft thud the door closed, as the engine spluttered to life.

Slowly the propellers began to turn, then faster and faster, slicing through the air. Soon they were invisible to all on board.

The engine droned louder, pulsating as Jocelyn pumped the aviation fuel. As she revved up the power, she turned to Jim and asked loudly, "Sumatra? You never did tell me why you want to go to Sumatra."

"Yes, Jim," added Doris. "Why Sumatra?"

"Quaaaoo?"

"Now *there's* a story," he said, smiling, as the plane rolled steadily across the compacted sand and gathered speed to lift it up into the great blueness of the upper realms.

SUBDUED CARGO

"PRESTON GLAMOURDUST? *Preston Glamourdust?* Where in all the world did you dredge *that* name from?"

Now that her rate of winged acceleration had been stopped completely, the smudge of feathers – otherwise known as Desdemona the raven – was sitting on the dashboard of the pantechnicon as it sped through the narrow alleyways and deserted streets that led to Istanbul's main shipping harbour.

She pecked at a flea that was nibbling into the flesh beneath her dull black feathers, then raised her beak. "Of all the outlandish names ... sheesh, I coulda done better in the name-makin'-up department!"

"I doubt that, you jealous jumble of juvenal jaundice. With your walnut of a brain, I doubt that very much indeed. Arrrr."

Captain Neptune F. Bone took a long puff on his Belch of Brouhaha cigar and exhaled the acrid, thick smoke straight at the bird.

"Oh, charming," she half-croaked, half-coughed, her red eyeballs throbbing even harder than they normally did. "That's a fine way to treat the only living creature who's stuck by you through thick and thin." She cast a slitted glance at his huge stomach jammed hard against

the steering wheel. "Or, perhaps in your case, I should say through thick and thicker."

"Enshut that drivelling beak of yours before I do the deed myself."

"Well, it's true," she rasped, shaking her left leg and sending twenty-two fleas springing onto the dashboard. "I've been with you through more harebrained schemes than I've had hot baths. You and you eternal lust for glory. Sheesh!"

"You're always free to fly away and leave me."

"Oh, yeah, *sure* I am. The Antiquities Squad the world over are hunting for you and me. I'm sure I'd last about two minutes if I didn't have your *huge* presence to hide behind."

"At least," rumbled the large and sweaty man, "you have seen parts of the world that most ordinary birds never even dream of." The tassel on his ochre-coloured fez swung against his eyes and, with a deft hand, he skewed the fez around to the right, so that the tassel bobbed against the back of his greasy head.

"Oh, yeah, thanks for remindin' me. Crark! How many other ravens could count themselves so lucky to have seen every single grain of sand by the pyramids on the Giza Plateau? Or to have smelled the dank, ancient pong of a disused store-room from a Turkish temple that's so old no one can even remember it?* Or to have

---

* See *Cairo Jim Amidst the Petticoats of Artemis –
A Turkish Tale of Treachery*

 3 3

been plummeted into the bottom of a Peruvian jungle valley?* Oh, yes indeedy, I am the luckiest, most fortunate, most abundantly blessed raven alive."

Bone turned the van around a tight corner, and the bird skidded across the dashboard and banged against the side window. "Sarcasm suits you about as much as the power of speech suits you. Which is a feather's breadth above not at all."

"Oof," she grunted, rubbing the back of her skullfeathers. "Are we nearly there yet?"

"You have indeed been fortunate," he said, his cigar sticking straight out from his flabby lips. "You have witnessed my many attempts at securing the recognition of this vast and stupid garbage dump we call 'civilisation'. You have been there each time I have almost alerted the world to my true qualities of unmitigated, brilliant Genius! Arrrr."

"And you've failed," she muttered, perching on the back of the passenger seat next to Bone. "Failed, failed, failed! Every single time."

In the blink of an eye, one of Bone's fists shot out from the steering wheel and connected with the back of the passenger seat, beneath where she was perched. The vibration sent her sprawling. She bounced off the seat and onto the floor.

"*Failed* is not a word that is synonymous with

---

* See *Cairo Jim on the Trail to ChaCha Muchos – An Epic Tale of Rhythm*

34

Neptune Flannelbottom Bone. Never forget that, Desdemona, or it is likely to be a costly mistake for you."

She picked herself up, shook out her feathers, and hopped up onto the seat, keeping a wary distance from his sudden bursts of anger. "And now," she whined, "we've got a truckload of huge, fierce Turkish women, all of 'em got by false pretendness. May I ask you a question, oh great Genius of my life?"

"What is it, you gormless glob of grunge?"

"What exactly do you want with eight Turkish Women's Olympic Championship Tent Erection Team members?"

"You'll see."

"It doesn't involve mud and jelly and wrestling, does it?"

Bone looked shocked. "Heavens to the Goddess Betsy, of course not! Where do such thoughts come from?"

"I'm a raven of the world," she said. "I get around."

Bone shuddered. "No, my procurement of those Turkish women does not involve what you mentioned. No, Desdemona, those huge, strong and resilient women are to become the helping-hands – or the helping glove-wearers, if you like – of my new scheme. My scheme to obtain some of the fortune that has hitherto eluded my illustrious self."

"Oh, brother," Desdemona muttered. "You've got so many big words comin' outta that gob of yours, it's a wonder you don't have a stretched gullet!"

"I shall ignore your wretched attempts at insults for

the time being and concentrate on my driving." His eyes glinted as he steered the pantechnicon up a steep lane.

"Are we nearly there yet?"

"Not far to go now."

A steady rain had begun to fall, and the windscreen was drizzling with many blurred streams of water. Bone turned on the windshield wipers and they screeched along the glass like the talons of a vulture skidding back and forth on a glassy surface in search of prey.

For several minutes the huge van lurched through a maze of dingy streets and shortcuts, sloshing through the quickly forming puddles in the cobblestones.

"HEY!" croaked Desdemona after a while.

"What, you blithering blurter?"

"Those women are awfully quiet back there. We haven't heard a peep outta them since we turned outta that first alley, way back when we womennapped 'em." Her red eyes glinted fiendishly with her hatred of women human beings. "D'ya think they're all *dead*? Maybe they went and suffer-cated?"

"No, Desdemona, they are not dead. If they were dead, then they would be entirely superfluous to my needs."

"And they wouldn't be much use, either. Then how come they're so quiet?"

"Two reasons, which, using my Genius Planning Methods and my Brilliance of Foresight, I arranged when I hired this pantechnicon."

"Yeah?"

"Arrr."

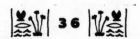

"Well, you gonna tell me, or am I just gonna sit here like a rock on a shag?"

"Reason One: this van is a *refrigerated* van. It is normally used for the transportation of frozen meats and the carcasses of dumb animals."

"Well, we got the right sorta van, then!"

"As soon as we drove off, after the Turkish Women's Olympic Championship Tent Erection Team had been secured in the back, I turned the refrigeration setting to its coldest level. That has slowed those women down … they have no energy to bang on the sides of the van or to try and rip through the wall behind us that separates our cabin from their icy domain. Arrrr."

"But won't they freeze to death?" There was hopefulness in her tone.

"I have thought of that, you doubting domicile of dumbness. No, it is only a short drive from their head-quarters to the ship upon which I have booked passage for our vehicle."

"Are we nearly there yet?"

"And, because it is only a short trip, there is not enough time for the women to freeze completely to death. No, by the time we arrive" – he whipped out his gold fob-watch from the pocket of his emerald-green waistcoat, and studied the dial – "which I estimate will be in two more minutes, the women will only be numbed. Chilled and numbed, just the way I need them."

"Ah," gurgled the raven, nodding at his foresight.

"And the second reason? What's the second reason why they've been so quiet?"

"Obsequious Gas."

"Obsequious Gas?"

"Arrr." The smoke curled up and out from his cigar and mingled through the hairs of his moustache and beard. "I have been piping a special gas through a small ventilation shaft just above your head. Obsequious Gas has only just been invented. It has never been available in shops, only through one of those infernal home-shopping channels on the television. That is how I bought the entire supply from the manufacturer."

"You *swindled* it, more like."

He puffed smugly on the cigar. "We should be safely out of the country before they discover that my cheque will bounce."

"So what does this Obsequious Gas do?"

"It seeps into the nostrils and then into the nervous system of all those who breathe it, and it renders those people totally under my power. They will obey me fully, and carry out whatever orders I give them. They will follow my wishes and desires without question. Oh, isn't that the dream of every discerning despot?"

"Well clone me and call me DoubleDes!"

"I knew you'd be impressed. Even I was slightly flabbergasted when I saw this gas advertised on the idiot box."

A young man on a bicycle appeared in their headlights. Bone swerved the van sharply, sloshing a river-load of water from a puddle all over the man and his bike.

"Watch where you're going, you stupid dreg!" Bone shouted angrily.

"Har-crark-har! Good one!"

"The imbecile," muttered Bone, puffing on his cigar. "The last thing I want is to have to stay in this rotten country on account of squashing some stupid cyclist. No, the sooner we're on the high seas, the better."

"Something has just occurred to me, my Captain."

"What? Have you forgotten who you are again?"

"No, no, no. But I've thought of something you haven't! Something that will upset your truffle-cart!"

"Oh, yes?"

"Yep."

"Pray, enlighten me, bird of brilliance."

"Well, what happens when we get those women outta the back of the truck? When they thaw out, and when they're no longer in a place where you can waft the Obsequious Gas all over 'em and up their nostrils? They won't be so eager to please you then, will they?"

"Oh, yes they will."

"How come? They'll have their own minds back, then. They'll be able to think for themselves again. From what I saw through the window back at their headquarters, when that really big woman picked you up by your collar and your eyeballs nearly burst, they'll make minced meat outta you."

"Why do you constantly underestimate me? Does not my forward-thinking ever rub off on you? Let me put it as simply as I can, so that your amoeba-like powers of snow-pea intellect may understand: I have thought of everything."

"So how?"

"It is true, what you say. As soon as we are on the open seas, and later on as well, when we are in wider, more sinister places, I shall turn off the refrigeration system and let them out of the van. When that happens, I shall resort to another product of which I purchased the world's entire supply: Obsequious *Pills*."

The raven looked at him, her eyes throbbing.

"I shall simply put the Obsequious Pills into their tea every morning – the women of the Turkish Women's Olympic Championship Tent Erection Team always start their day with several cups of strong, piping-hot Turkish tea – and they will continue to obey me, morning, noon and night. They will still do whatever I instruct them to do."

"You're inspired, you are."

"Thank you, my faithful fiend. Arrr, look, there's the signpost to the dock, where our ship will be waiting."

He steered over to the side of the road, and idled the engine.

"Why're you stopping here?" asked Desdemona.

Bone reached under his seat and pulled out a large wooden crate with a little door in one end. "I just wanted to get your supply of tinned Japanese seaweed ready for you before we drove the vehicle on board."

"Tinned Japanese seaweed? Oh, you shouldn't have! You know how much I love ... wait a momentum, you've never bought me tinned Japanese seaweed before.

Usually I have ta go and steal it. How come—?"

"To make your voyage a little more pleasurable," Bone purred. "Go on, see how many tins I got for you. They're in the crate."

She hopped to the door of the crate and peered in. "Hey, hang on, there're no—SCREEEEEEEER-AAAAAARK!"

With a flurry of his fist, Bone shoved her inside the crate and slammed the door shut, whacking an enormous padlock onto a latch. "Don't try to splinter the wood, Desdemona, it has an inner core of tungsten steel. I'm sure you'll be able to make yourself comfortable, and it's only for three days. If the weather holds up and our course is a smooth one."

"But why?" she spat. "We've always travelled together. Why the crate?"

"Because," he answered, putting the crate on the passenger seat and steering the truck towards the dock, "there is only one first-class cabin, and I wanted that all for myself. Your odour is nauseating at the best of times, and at the other times – which is *most* times – I would rather gnaw off my own earlobes than have to smell you in confined quarters such as a ship's cabin."

"Nevermore, nevermore, nevermore!" She slumped against the reinforced wooden slats.

"There's our ship: the SS *Ruby Keeler*. Arrrr. You, along with the women, will be travelling inside the pantechnicon in the cargo hold. I will turn off the refrigeration as soon as the vehicle is secured beneath decks, and don't fret: it's only for three days, and I shall visit you every morning when I serve the women their tea."

"Three days? Where on earth are we sailin' to in three days?"

"As I have told you on at least a thousand occasions, time will reveal all. Arrrrrrrrrr!"

◎ ◎ ◎ ◎ ◎ **4** ◎ ◎ ◎ ◎ ◎

THE LEGACY OF DR SCHNITGER

THE SKY STRETCHED before the Lockheed Vega like the thickest and softest of blue quilts, interlaced every now and then with gentle wisps of pure white cloud.

In the cockpit, Jocelyn surveyed the gentle expanse ahead. She had decided to fly over Cairo, across the Middle East and India and thence to Sumatra. This was not exactly the shortest route – it would have been quicker to cross the oceans and seas – but she figured it would be the safest. Her aircraft, after all, was only a recent purchase, and she still wasn't completely familiar with all the little foibles of a second-hand plane such as this. If there were to be any mechanical problems, Jocelyn would rather be over land, where she could down the plane with greater chance of safety than if they were flying above water.

The propellers droned steadily, but not loudly enough to be a discomfort; it was still possible to have a conversation above the noise without shouting so much your face or feathers went red. For Brenda, the noise was no bother at all – she had snouted out her Melodious Tex Western adventure novel and was happily immersing herself in Tex's exploits in the dry and barren land of Rancid Ravine.

 43

"So, Jim," Jocelyn said as the River Nile flowed far beneath, "tell us about Sumatra."

"Rark! Enlighten us!"

"Well," he said, reaching down and delving into his knapsack which lay between his feet, "I got the idea of going there from a short article I read recently. It was in the latest issue of *Thoth's Blurter*."

"*Thoth's Blurter*?" Jocelyn raised her eyebrows behind her flying goggles.

"It's the official magazine of the Old Relics Society," Doris told her in something of an important tone. "Only Members of the Society see it."

"Oh." Jocelyn smiled. There were many things she didn't know about the Old Relics Society, on account of her not being a Member.

"Here it is." Jim pulled out a folded, glossy magazine from the knapsack. He unfolded it and showed Jocelyn and Doris the cover.

"I know that face," Jocelyn observed.

"Of course you do," said Jim.

The cover of the magazine featured a large, head-and-shoulders photo of an elderly man with a neat, black moustache and twinkling, possum-like eyes.

"Gerald Perry Esquire," commented the Valkyrian. "Your loyal patron."

"Mm-hm," Cairo Jim nodded.

"Rerk! He's on the cover *again*!"

"Yes," said Jim, "he seems to get himself on it often, doesn't he?"

Jocelyn laughed. "Never one to miss out on an opportunity."

Doris blinked at the photo. "He hasn't looked *that* young in twenty years!"

"They've touched him up," Jocelyn told her.

Doris's feathers bristled at the thought. She was glad she wasn't the subject of magazine covers – if anyone tried to touch *her* up, there'd be feathers aflying.

Jim opened the magazine and began flipping through it.

"Has Perry sent us to Sumatra on another expedition?" Doris asked, flexing her wings slightly. "Is this his doing?"

"No, not this time."

"Then what gave you the idea?"

The archaeologist-poet found the page he was looking for, and folded the magazine back so it could be seen clearly. "See? The regular feature on Members Who Dug Before Us. This month it's about Doctor Schnitger."

"Doctor Schnitger!" squawked Doris excitedly. "Doctor Schnitger!"

"Doctor Friedrich Schnitger."

"Doctor Friedrich Schnitger! Rark rark rark!" She started bobbing up and down between Jocelyn and Jim.

"You know of him, my dear?"

She stopped bobbing, and blinked. "Actually, no. Never heard of him."

Jocelyn smiled at the macaw's exuberance.

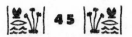

"No," Jim said. "Not many people or macaws today *have* heard of him."

"Quaoooo," came a snort from the rear of the plane.

"Or Wonder Camels," Jim added. "No, you see, it's been decades since Dr Schnitger wrote of his discoveries in Sumatra. He uncovered lots there – many ancient burial sites and great granite statues of Buddha and stone terraces and exquisite bronze artefacts and ruined temples – but there was *one* discovery he made that seems shrouded in secrecy…"

He paused, letting the drone of the propellers and the steady hum of the engine carry his words through the aircraft's interior.

"Go on," Jocelyn urged after a few seconds. "What was it?"

"Well, according to this Members Who Dug Before Us article, Schnitger had been excavating in Sumatra for eight years when he made the most important dicovery of his career: high on a flat-topped mountain in the ranges of Bukit Barisan, south-west of the city of Palembang, completely covered by dense and almost impenetrable jungle, he found a vast and beautiful Palace."

"A Palace?" blinked Doris.

"A Royal Palace dating back to the year 683. It was built by the Maharaja of Srivijaya, the most powerful ruler of his time."

"Srivijaya," Doris cooed.

"In those days, the area around Palembang and into the mountains was the hub of a great empire which controlled the trading routes all through the area we know as India, Malaysia and China."

"What was the Palace like?" Jocelyn asked eagerly – archaeology was her number-one hobby, and she loved it just as much as Flight Attending, which was her living.

"Now *that*," replied Cairo Jim, "is what makes this so intriguing. In his notes, Schnitger described the jungle, and the arduous trekking he and his equipment-bearers had to do to get to the top of the mountain, but after that, his pen went very quiet. We have no description of what the Palace of Srivijaya looked like, except for general things Schnitger wrote, like … let me see…"

They waited as he read through the article.

"Ah, listen to this: 'According to Dr Schnitger, the Palace of the Maharaja was

'… The most splendid, the most beautiful, the most stupendous and lavish of any ancient monuments I have had the pleasure to uncover. But the beauty of the place is not what makes it outstanding. No, there is something else about the Palace of Srivijaya, something that went on during the Maharaja's reign that made this Palace and its grounds the most amazing and unbelievable location of its time. Indeed, of its time and any time since, for nothing that I will ever discover during my days on this Earth will surpass the astonishing spectacle that surrounds the Palace of Srivijaya, and which makes it all so unique.'"

Jim stopped reading, and stared out into the wide, limitless skies.

"What?" prerked Doris impatiently. "What was it that made the Palace so special, so amazing?"

"Yes, Jim, what was it?"

"Quaaooo?" snorted Brenda, who had stopped reading her novel when Jim had started reading from *Thoth's Blurter*.

"Schnitger wouldn't say," Jim answered at last. "Listen." He started reading again from the magazine:

"'Dr Schnitger never wrote what it was that made the Palace so astonishing and unique. According to the last report he wrote about it:

But I will never tell another outsider what it is that makes this location so magnificent, and so valuable, to archaeologists and to the modern world alike. I have taken an oath of secrecy with the local peoples who live below the mountain. They never venture up to this place, believing that History should be left to dwell within its own time and natural evolution. Normally I would argue with this, but, because of the exceptional and amazing circumstances that have surrounded the Palace of Srivijaya for nearly 1300 years, I agree with them entirely.

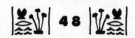

And so my pen rests, and with it, I hope, rests the site of the Maharaja's Palace. May plunderers never uncover its extraordinary secret.'"

Jim closed the magazine and, just as had happened the first time and every other time he had read the article, a huge shiver of excitement shot down his spine.

"Fascinating," Jocelyn smiled, her skin, too, erupting in a series of bold but not embarrassing goose-bumps.

"Oh, thank goodness for the mysteries of the world," Doris crowed, her crestfeathers arching forward. "How Time does cover 'the forms of things unknown'," she said, quoting from Shakespeare's *A Midsummer Night's Dream*.

"Quaaoo," snorted the Wonder Camel, her mane tingling with anticipation.

"What happened to Dr Schnitger, Jim?" enquired Jocelyn.

"World War Two," answered Jim. "The War interrupted many things, including Dr Schnitger's work. What happened to him after that, I have no idea…"

"Intriguing," Jocelyn said, turning her attention once again to the skies ahead.

Jim put the magazine back into his knapsack and Doris hopped up onto his lap. "D'you think we'll manage to find the Palace of Srivijaya?" she asked, her small eyes bright with the possibility.

"Well, we'll give it a shot, won't we?"

"Raark."

"Of course, if we *are* lucky enough to find it, we won't be taking anything away with us. We'll just record it by taking photos – I have one of Pyrella Frith's★ cameras which she kindly lent me – and by taking measurements and making notes, and we'll deposit our findings in the library at the Old Relics Society. We must respect the wishes of Dr Schnitger and the Sumatrans who trusted him."

Suddenly Jocelyn laughed – a light, hearty laugh that filled the cockpit.

"What's the joke?" asked Doris.

"Oh, no joke." Jocelyn beamed at the brightness ahead. "It's just that it doesn't seem like much of a holiday for you, Jim. You'll still be up to your elbows in trying to find the ancient past."

Jim liked her turn of phrase. "I guess so. But it's a change of scenery, isn't it? And the Palace isn't as ancient as most of the sites or artefacts we've been after. So that's a bit of a change as well."

"Plus there's a real mystery here," Doris chipped in. "Just think … if we're all able to solve *that*, and find out what Dr Schnitger wouldn't write about!"

"Quaoooo," snorted Brenda.

★ The talented archaeological photographer who assists Cairo Jim in *Cairo Jim in Search of Martenarten* and *Cairo Jim and the Quest for the Quetzal Queen.*

"That's *my* idea of a holiday," Jim said quietly, as he watched the clouds rolling and threading in front of him.

The ocean gloomed like a neverending oil slick, dark and fathomless and murky, and the sun slid dismally over the horizon.

Deep within the bowels of the SS *Ruby Keeler*, in the only first-class passenger cabin on the whole ship, Neptune Bone was snoring on a moth-eaten divan beneath the cabin's single porthole.

On the table next to him were the remains of seven Belzoni Whopper cocktails, which Bone had drunk since leaving the port of Istanbul, and one undrunk Belzoni Whopper. Next to all the glasses an ashtray was overflowing with Belch of Brouhaha cigar stubs and ash. He had smoked a lot in the last two days, and the cabin reeked.

On the floor was an empty copper samovar (in which he brewed the special tea that he took down to the hold at regular intervals for the Turkish women), and his substantial Louis Vuitton Travelling Trunkette.

Bone gurgled and emitted a loud snort. It blasted out from his nostrils like a claggy gunshot. He licked his lips and settled further into his slumber.

The SS *Ruby Keeler* lurched on a big swell in the ocean, and the cabin rose into the air.

"What the—?" Bone spluttered, roused from his sleep by the feeling of his stomach dropping away from him. He opened his eyes as the ship lurched again, and stared up at the stained ceiling. "Blasted boat," he grumbled. "Next time I'll take the *Ginger Rogers*."

The overblown man stretched his legs and wiggled his sausage-like toes (he had kicked off his spats and stockings, and they lay in a messy heap in the corner). His antique manicure set slid off his lap (he had been buffing his fingernails before he had fallen asleep), and clattered onto the floor.

He rolled over a bit, grunted, and pulled out from the back pocket of his plus-fours trousers a grubby, black, leather-bound pocket-journal. Around the small book was an old rubber band.

Having got the journal, he rolled back again, his wide bottom spreading across the divan like two mammoth balloons full of jelly.

He slid the rubber band off the journal and opened the book. His eyes lit up as he re-read the entry he had made three weeks earlier.

"Arrr," he muttered. "Yes, yes, yes. All shall be mine. Amazing where a little bit of initiative will lead a man!"

He flicked through the pages to the back of the journal. Here he had slipped a folded map and now he pulled it out and slowly unfolded it on his knees.

As the island on the map emerged beneath his gaze, he reached out and picked up his eighth Belzoni Whopper. "To Sumatra," he toasted, raising the glass. "And all that Schnitger failed to tell us! *Arrrrrrr*!"

DOWN TO EARTH

DORIS WAS HAVING the strangest dream.

She knew she was airborne, yet she couldn't feel her wings moving. Nor could she feel her feathers being ruffled by the breezes that always cooled her when she was in the air. And there was no wind blowing against her eyes and beak. Yet she knew that she was somehow flying, further and further, far and away…

And there was the noise. Here in her sleep she was constantly aware of it: a droning, as if she were being escorted by a procession of earnest mosquitoes who were everywhere around her, yet not too close to cramp her space.

"Doris!"

A voice, soft, gentle and calming, was coming from somewhere out there…

"Doris, my dear! Wake up! Look what's below!"

The macaw jerked her beak up. She opened her eyes and blinked rapidly four times. It was Jim, and she was on his thigh, nestled in against his stomach. She looked around and remembered where she was.

"Rark. I must've gone sleepies," she muttered.

"You've been out for over six hours," Jocelyn told her.

"I think not!" remonstrated Doris.

"You have, my dear." Jim ruffled the feathers on her chest. "Hasn't she, Brenda?"

"Quaaaooo," snorted the Wonder Camel, rolling her head.

"Must've needed it," Doris said.

"Look, down there." Jim lifted her to his shoulder, and the bird peered down through the thinning carpet of clouds.

Far below, a huge line of mountains stretched away. Every inch of the mountains was covered in green – the thick, dense, dark green of tropical jungle.

Faint plumes of mist and steam rose up like spindly, spectral fingers, from deep ravines half-smothered by the lush vegetation.

"Sumatra," announced Jim. "We flew over Palembang about an hour ago."

"And now we're flying towards the mountains," thought Brenda. *"The tangled mountains of Bukit Barisan."*

"And now we're flying towards the mountains," said Jocelyn, picking up on the Wonder Camel's thought. "The tangled mountains of Bukit Barisan."

"Which is where Schnitger wrote that he found the Palace." Doris flexed herself up and down, but then stopped. "But which mountain?"

"One that's flat-topped," Jim said. He shifted Doris to the side and, reaching down, pulled out a large map of south-western Sumatra and his To the Ends of the Earth & All the Realms In-Between Archaeological Compass.

Jocelyn turned the plane to the south and decreased the altitude, so that they were, in less than a minute, passing through stringy threads of vaporous, rain-filled clouds. "I'm taking us down a bit," she told Jim, Doris and Brenda, "so that these clouds don't obscure our view."

"Good thinking."

Doris rummaged around in Jim's knapsack, and dragged out her own pair of binoculars. She arranged these on top of the control panel, in front of Jim, and she positioned herself so that she could see comfortably through one of the eyepieces.

Brenda had shut her book and had moved her humps around so that she had an unrestricted view out of two of the rear windows. Her eyes big and alert, she scanned the mountains below, trying to see deep into the tree-studded chasms and misty ravines.

"Okay," Jocelyn said after a few minutes. "This looks like where the Bukit Barisans begin."

She turned the Lockheed back towards the north-east, and slowly began to follow the line of the mountain range.

The peaks were haphazard, alternating between high, jagged, tree-covered pinnacles and lower, gentler mountains that were nestled between the higher reaches. Many of the lower mountains were covered with massive tree-ferns, and dotted with bright colours – reds and yellows, oranges and purples – from flowering vines and plants that threaded through all the greenery.

A light drizzle began to fall as the plane followed the mountain chain. Soon the aircraft was surrounded by a thin sheet of shifting droplets. Every now and then the sunshine from above speared through the droplets, and a brilliant golden light shone all around the plane.

Cairo Jim followed the progress of the mountains against his map.

Onwards flew the plane, sometimes dipping closer to the lower rises, but always rising again to avoid the looming cliffs and tree-lined outcrops.

Onwards stretched the range, high and low, washed in the gentle rain and then bathed in the glowing sunlight. Glistening leaves and fronds and dripping boughs appeared like a massive carpet of untouched beauty.

Onwards crept Cairo Jim's desire to find out more about Dr Schnitger's mysterious Palace of Srivijaya.

Then Brenda the Wonder Camel gave a snort – a snort of discovery!

"QUUUAAAAAAAAAAAAAAAAAAAOOOOOOO!"

"My lovely!" Jim swivelled in his seat. "What've you seen?"

She rolled her head and flickered her eyelashes downwards, using them to signal out the port window.

"Rark! Turn the plane to port, Jocelyn Osgood!"

"Roger, Doris the macaw!" Smiling, Jocelyn pulled back on the joystick and slowly, gradually, the plane turned towards the left.

Jim peered down through the curtain of raindrops.

"Brenda, you clever beast of Wonder! Look, everyone, down there at eleven o'clock!"

Down to the left, rising higher than the surrounding peaks, towered a wide, flattish expanse of trees. It looked as if some giant had come through with a pair of scissors and had neatly trimmed the area, but had left all the surrounding mountains wild and unkempt.

Doris blinked through the binoculars. "I'd say underneath all those trees and jungle, there's a plateau."

Quickly, Jim looked at his map. "Swoggle me skywards. You'll never guess!"

"What, Jim?"

"Rerk, what, Jim?"

"Quaaoo, quaoo?"

"On the map, what we see below is marked as 'Gunung Dempo'. It's a dormant volcano. The map says it's 3159 metres above sea level."

"A dormant volcano," repeated Jocelyn thoughtfully.

"And volcanoes," said Jim quietly, "are always flat on top, within the crater."

Jocelyn frowned. "Too dense to make a landing there, though. Too many trees."

"Joss, can we take a closer look? Let's fly up and down the side."

"As good as done."

For the next twenty minutes, at a steady, confident pace at the steady, confident hand of Jocelyn Osgood, the plane flew close to Gunung Dempo. The side of the extinct volcano was steep, and thick with growth.

Every so often a bare expanse of hard, dark rock-face would be visible, but mostly the volcano was smothered in rampant greenery.

Then Doris screeched excitedly. "There! At three o'clock! See, a track!"

"Good work, Doris. See it, Joss?"

"I see it."

"Quaooo," came a snort from the back.

Snaking up Gunung Dempo was the unmistakable outline of a rough track. Sometimes it disappeared beneath overhanging trees, but it always emerged again, and continued all the way – or so it looked – to near the top of the mountain, where the plants and huge branches covered it completely.

Mostly the track appeared wide enough for two people to walk up side by side, but not always; in places it dwindled and narrowed, until it was little more than a stretch of exposed mud clinging to the very edge of the volcano. In all of these narrower places, there was very little vegetation – the escarpments were walls of dark, glistening rock: bold, stark and barren.

"It's heavily overgrown here and there," observed Jim. "But I think we'll be able to manage." He flipped open the lid of his compass and began to jot the bearings of the track down in the margin of his map.

"Let's take a look at the top again, Joss. See if we can find where the track comes out."

"Rightio." She pulled back on the joystick and up they rose.

Now that they were once again above the volcano, things looked different. The drizzle had almost stopped, and the sun was gilding the leaves of the canopy that covered the plateau in a bold, yellow glow.

"That'd be the crater under all that growth."

Doris looked puzzled. "The crater? Seems like a strange place to build a Palace, in the crater of a volcano."

"It does, doesn't it?"

Brenda had been studying the leaves in the trees of the canopy that obliterated their view, and now she sent out a thought: "Look! The trees down there! Their leaves are a different colour to all the trees that grow up the side of the volcano!"

"Jim!" blurted Jocelyn. "Look at the trees down there! Their leaves are a different colour to all the trees that grow up the side of the volcano!"

Jim and Doris craned their heads and looked down.

"I've never seen foliage like that before," muttered the archaeologist-poet.

"Me neither," said Doris. ""'Tis strange, 'tis very strange'," she added, quoting from *All's Well That Ends Well*.

"So much brighter," Jocelyn said quietly.

"And it's not just because of the sun," Brenda thought. *"There's something else …"*

Jim took off his special desert sun-spectacles and looked again. "Those leaves and fronds. They seem to be … *glimmering*."

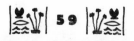 59

"They do," Jocelyn agreed. Then she looked at the control panels and frowned. "Jim, Doris, Brenda, we're running low on fuel. I'm going to have to put us down in the foothills over there. I've seen some open fields or something – I think it's a tea-growing area, by the looks of things. Should be suitable for a landing."

"Whatever you say," answered Jim, his attention still firmly fixed on the strange growth. His archaeological instincts rose up. "There's something under all those giant ferns and colossal trees, I'm sure of it."

Jocelyn was turning the plane, preparing for a smooth descent, when she gasped, quietly, but suddenly enough to startle everyone on board.

BLIND DEVOTION

"OH!" JOCELYN GASPED AGAIN.

It was only a small gasp, like the first one, but Jim turned immediately to look at her. She had pulled her hands from the joystick and was holding them across her flying-goggles.

"Joss! What's wrong?"

"Jim, I – I can't see!"

"What?"

"Raaark!" Doris cocked her head, her plumage wild with concern.

"Quaaaaaooo?"

"I can't see! There was a bolt of light or something. Bright, too bright. It shot up from below, from the trees, down there, all yellow, *too* yellow, shot straight into my goggles and—"

"Joss, the plane!"

The aircraft was tilting downwards, its nose pointing first towards the side of Gunung Dempo and then, in a horrifying matter of seconds, swerving further, swiftly around in the direction of the foothills.

The plane was aimed directly at the ground, and the ground was speeding upwards with a dizzying, sickening velocity!

 61

"Quick, Jim, grab the joystick! Do exactly as I—"

There was a spluttering, loud, desperate, frantic AKKATAAKKAAKAAAAKKKKKAAAA!

And then the propellers stopped, with a dreadful coughing sound and a loud wheeze.

"The props have gone!" shouted Jim. "We're plummeting faster!"

The plane screamed through the air.

"We're diving!" Doris screeched at the top of her lungs.

Second by second, the jungle below was getting closer and closer...

"Jim, listen to me!" Jocelyn's voice was calm, but loud and dominant. "I said: take the joystick!"

He reached over and did so.

"Now pull back!" she ordered. "We've lost all power, and we can't start again – not enough fuel! We have to coast down to those tea fields I saw earlier. See them?"

Jim craned his neck and looked wildly down. The jungle was blurring as it neared, and the screaming air turbulence was almost deafening as they dropped. "Yes! Over to the" – he glanced at the aircraft compass – "east!"

"Pull around, steadily!"

His palms sweating as if waterfalls were spilling out from them, he tightened his grip on the joystick and pulled it hard to the east. The plane bumped against the air outside, but began to point in the right direction.

"How close till the ground?" Jocelyn shouted.

"Couple of thousand feet," Jim shouted back.

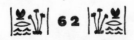

"Push the joystick towards the centre of the cockpit!" yelled Jocelyn.

Jim's sweaty hand pushed the joystick. The nose of the aircraft rose, and in two seconds the plane was no longer pointing down, but was level with the oncoming ground. But now they were losing altitude faster!

"Look carefully, Jim, Doris, Brenda. Is there any open area where the ground looks like it's compacted hard? Some place that's not swampy or overgrown?"

Brenda snorted loudly, and Doris looked where she had seen.

"Down there, to the right! A roadway."

"I see it!" cried Jim. "Earth, not tarred. But it looks firm."

"Bring her round, bring her round," Doris muttered frantically.

"Take us level with it, Jim," shouted Jocelyn, still unable to see anything except a yellow gleam whenever she opened her eyes. "How long is the road?"

"Very long. Long enough for a runway." Then he added, under his breath, "I hope."

The ground was rising higher and higher as lower and lower they fell...

The air had stopped screaming at them, but it was now humming – deeply, loudly, getting louder by the second...

"Follow the road," Jocelyn hollered. "And gradually bring us close!"

"Rightio!"

The plane was shooting through the airspace above the road, its wings tilting wildly up and down.

"Keep it steady, Jim! Watch the wings!"

"I'm trying," he grunted, straightening the joystick.

"Doris, listen carefully: locate the knob on the control panel that has 'wheels' written on it."

"Rerk, found it!"

"Pull it out with your beak, all the way, NOW!"

She leant forward and yanked the knob fully out. There was a loud *clunk* from under the fuselage as the landing wheels dropped down.

Beneath them, the rough road was flashing by in a frenzy of speed.

"Now, Jim, steady descent. Imagine you're slowly closing a very heavy lid on a trunk, just push the stick like that!"

"Here goes!"

The wings wobbled as he pushed the joystick forward. In the rear, Brenda slid and bumped against the side of the plane.

The road stretched under them, the dirt in it dark and blurred.

Doris clamped a wing over her eyes.

Jocelyn shut her eyes tightly to avoid the yellow light.

Brenda held her breath until her humps started to tingle.

And Cairo Jim thought of poetry, as slowly, jerkily, the wheels hit the roadway.

BERDDDDNNNNNNNKKKKKKKKKKKKK!

Everything vibrated wildly: the cabin, the cockpit, the wings and dead propellers, the ribcages of Jim, Jocelyn, Doris and Brenda. The macaw's feathers jittered as fiercely if she had been standing in front of an industrial-strength electric fan.

The Lockheed sped and juddered wildly down the roadway, the wheels screeching and the plane bumping over potholes and ridges.

"Now," shouted Jocelyn, "PULL BACK, AS FAR AS YOU CAN!"

Jim wrenched the joystick backwards until it pressed hard against Jocelyn's stomach. Gradually, as time spun all around them, the aircraft began to slow.

"That's it," Jocelyn said. "Nice and—"

"Scraaaaarrrrrrrkkkkkkk! The road! There's no more! Look out!"

Ahead of them, looming out from the distance like a dark, impenetrable fist, was an enormous pile of massive boulders and hardened lava which had long ago rolled and poured down from the volcano.

"No!" cried Jim. They were slowing, but were still travelling far too fast to avoid a collision that would reduce the plane to matchsticks. "Joss, I'm sorry, I've got to detour!"

He wrenched the joystick towards him, and the plane screamed around, turning so sharply that their stomachs were left momentarily behind.

The left wing smashed hard against the boulders.

With an ear-splitting CRACK it was ripped clean off the fuselage.

But the remainder of the plane had cleared the obstacle, and was now bounding uncontrollably across the foothills, bumping and bouncing across the thick grasses and small bushes and wet, puddly swampy areas.

"Hang on, everyone!" Jim steered the plane as best he could, trying to prevent it from overturning, attempting to keep the balance despite the loss of the wing.

The grasses were thicker, the bushes denser, the swampy holes thicker. Through it all the plane rocked and sped and sludged. Finally it skidded onto its side, the side that had lost the wing, and, totally out of control, with a huge BANG it slammed into the trunk of an immense ironwood tree.

The impact of the collision was so colossal, the noise so deafening, that it seemed as if all the world had splintered savagely apart.

From the nearby forest, a family of proboscis monkeys watched all of this with great interest. When the plane finally became dead-still against the tree, and the last, battered propeller blade had stopped turning, the leader of the group – an old, wizened male – shook his droopy nose in the air.

Then he led his family deeper into the dense safety of the treetops.

GLAMOURDUST
REVEALS A TAD

"LISTEN," WHISPERED Fatimé Breeches throatily to her Teammates in the back of the pantechnicon. "It seems we are moving."

The Turkish Women's Olympic Championship Tent Erection Team sat very still, and felt the motion of the van. It was a different sort of motion to the motion they had been feeling for the past few days: now, instead of rolling and swaying, the vehicle seemed to be moving forward and tilting slightly.

"You are right, Fatimé." Dënise stood and ran her huge palms against the inside wall. "We are going ahead, somewhere."

"We are moving down a ramp, I should think," Fatimé told them.

"Mr Glamourdust must be taking us somewhere new," said Osmana.

"Mr Glamourdust," repeated Kaynarca, her eyes wide and strangely dreamy.

"Mr Glamourdust," echoed the other women, their eyes similarly inflicted.

Dënise smiled. "What a lovely man he is. There is *nothing* I would not do for that fellow."

"Me too," agreed Osmana. "And he makes such beautiful tea, does he not?"

The darkness was thick, the night starless as Neptune Bone drove the pantechnicon away from the port of Krui, south-west of the volcano Gunung Dempo.

The van's headlights cast feeble beams onto the rough street ahead. Bone puffed earnestly on his cigar as he tried to negotiate the black uncertainty.

"Please, my Captain?" whined Desdemona from inside the steel-reinforced crate. "Please can I come out now?"

"All in good time," he sneered. On the seat next to him he had laid out the map of Sumatra which he had taken from the back of his grubby pocket-journal. He tried to consult the map as he drove along the dimly lit streets, but the lack of light was making the task impossible.

There was no question: he needed the raven's assistance.

"Listen to me, Desdemona. If I am to let you out, will you promise to respect me?"

"I promise, I promise, I promise!" Her red eyeballs throbbed malevolently behind the slats.

"And no more of your snide remarks?"

"Not one, not one, not one!"

"And you won't flick your fleas at me when I'm sleeping?"

"Nevermore, nevermore, never—"

"Yes, you've made your point, you repetitive rabble of redundancy."

"Can I come out then?"

"Arrr." He flicked some cigar ash out the open window and then withdrew his gold fob-watch chain from the pocket of his emerald-green waistcoat. Hanging on the chain was the key to the padlock on the crate.

Deftly, the turgid man manoeuvred his hand – keeping the other on the steering wheel – and inserted the key into the padlock. He twisted his wrist and the lock sprang open with a clunk.

In a flurry of seconds, Desdemona flung open the door and shot out of the crate, banging her beak into the passenger-door handle. "Oooooooooof!" she gasped, falling back onto the seat.

"Welcome back to the land of the civilised and free," Bone said in a voice dripping with sarcasm.

She pecked at a convention of fleas under her left wing, then spat most of the delegates out onto the dashboard. "If you ever do that to me again," she seethed, her chestfeathers rising and falling with three days' worth of confined fury, "if you ever shove me in any sorta cage or box or handbag, I'll ... I'll..."

"You'll what, you threatening thought-free thingummy?"

"I'll have yer toes for breakfast!"

His eyes glinted at her, flashing angrily. But only for a second – he had other, more important things to deal with at the moment. The raven could wait.

"Where are we?" she asked, hopping up onto the dashboard and staring out the windscreen at the deserted, dark streets and laneways.

"We are leaving the market district of Krui."

"Krui? Where in the name of Myrna Loy is that? Where are we?"

"On the island of Sumatra. South-west Sumatra, if you want to be exact."

"Sumatra?" she croaked.

"Arrrrrr."

She looked at him, then at the roadway, then at him again. "Is this where you're gonna obtain some of the fortune that has hitherto deluded your illustrated self?" She had – almost – remembered his words from three days previous; there had not been much else to think about, cooped up in that crate.

"It is, arrrr." He handed a small silver object to her. "Here, Desdemona, take my cigar-lighter and shine its light above the map on the seat there. I need to see which direction to take once we leave these ramshackle, pathetic markets."

She obeyed, being careful not to singe her feathertips.

Bone slowed the van and it moved through the street like an enormous, lugubrious slug. He kept one slitted eye on the map. "There, that's the direction we should take. All right, close the lighter, and keep your eyes peeled for a sign out there somewhere." The van picked up speed, and continued.

"A sign? What, like a finger pointing down from the heavens? Or a burning shrub? Or a shooting star?"

"No, you daft dollop of denseness. We may live in a very peculiar world, but it's not *that* far-fetched. No, a *street* sign. One that will point us in the direction of the Bukit Barisan mountains."

"Bukit Barisan," she repeated, and then promptly forgot the name. "HEY!"

Bone shuddered at her squawk. "What?"

"Tell me why we're here! What sort of wealth are you after in them mountains?"

"Look in the glove compartment." He blew a thick column of smoke straight at her.

When she had finished coughing, she leaned down and thumped the glove-compartment door sharply with her beak. The door fell open instantly. She poked her beak inside and pulled out a small black-and-white photograph, soiled at the edges.

"Hello, hello, hello? What have we here?" She flicked open the cigar lighter and a small flame whooshed out of it. By the light of the flame she inspected the photo. "Scrark! Yergh! When was this taken?"

Bone frowned curiously. "Whatever are you—?" Then, realising what the bird had in her talon, he reached out and snatched it away from her. "You didn't see that, Desdemona. Do you hear me?"

"Ha-crark-ha! I saw it, all right! Hergh hergh hergh. I never knew you were such a devotee of sword swallowing! Nice swimsuit! C'mon, who is she?"

"She is nobody," seethed the fatty man.

"And I'm Kylie Minogue!"

"She is merely an artiste of the theatre I happen to have come across recently. Her name is Nerida Ziggurat. She earns an amazing amount of money, doing what she does."

"Ha! Some *artiste*. I wish someone'd pay *me* to shove cutlery down my throat. Sheesh!"

"Forget you ever saw it, Desdemona, I'm warning you. Or else you'll become savagely acquainted with the undersole of my shoe."

"Screrk."

"That wasn't what you were supposed to find in the glove compartment." He tucked the photo into his waistcoat pocket. "Look again."

She blinked at him, then lowered her head. Once more her beak scrabbled about inside the compartment. When she pulled it out, there was a single sheet of glossy, printed paper in it.

She dropped it on the dashboard in front of her and lit the flame. "A bit of paper from some magazine," she said. "So what?"

"It's from *Thoth's Blurter*," Bone explained. "It's an article about the once-famous but now-forgotten archaeologist and Hindu relics expert, Dr Friedrich Schnitger."

"Schnitger," repeated the raven.

"It tells briefly of the Palace of Srivijaya, one of Schnitger's major discoveries. But it doesn't tell us *all*."

"Nope?"

"No. There were things Schnitger wouldn't tell about this Palace – amazing things, if we are to go by the tone of his writings. *Mysterious* things. When I read the article last month, my instincts rose up and told me that these things must be extremely *valuable*!"

"Ah ha!"

"And," Bone continued, his eyes filling with the delight of his own importance as he puffed indulgently on his Belch of Brouhaha, "my instincts were correct. One hundred per cent correct, as so often happens with a Genius such as what I am. And, as quite frequently occurs when instinct of Genius takes root, another thing waltzed along to me, to go hand-in-hand with this important instinct: the memory of an association!"

"Eh?" She squinted at him.

"I remembered that I had come across another piece in this Schnitger jigsaw puzzle, many years ago, when I was a young student at Archaeology School. A woman who knew Dr Schnitger very, very well. Her name was" – he inhaled the smoke deeply, and blew it out, all across the inside of the windscreen – "Lillian Bingal!"

CLOSER TO ARRIVAL, WHILE OTHERS WAIT...

"LILLIAN BINGAL?"

"Arrr."

They had left the market precinct, and were now heading out of town, into the country. Gradually the street lights at the sides of the road became fewer and a long way between, until they finally stopped altogether. Now, on this almost starless night, there were only the headlamps of the pantechnicon to light the road ahead.

"Go on," croaked Desdemona. "Tell me about her."

"As I said, she was a close friend of Schnitger from way back. I remembered – it was a typical stroke of the Genius that I am – I remembered, quite out of the bluish haze of the past, that when I was a student at Archaeology School, way back when I was younger—"

"—and when you looked more like a normal human being, instead of a dirigible with legs!"

He clenched his cigar between his teeth, and his beard bristled. "If I weren't engaged in driving this vehicle, you would be a squashed and sorry raven. Shut up and let me continue."

Her eyes throbbed redly as she stared out through the windscreen.

"I recalled that one day at Archaeology School, Lillian Bingal came along to give us a lecture about the work of Dr Friedrich Schnitger. It was most illuminating, although I didn't catch the *whole* lecture... I had to leave early, to take Mother to the Beauty Parlour and to sell some of my fake ancient scarabs to a bus load of rather dim but enthusiastic New Zealand tourists who had come to gawp at the Pyramids.

"But I *did* catch the general upshot of what Lillian Bingal was saying. She told us that Schnitger had spent his entire working life excavating in the jungles of Sumatra, where he had uncovered many remarkable statues, pieces of pottery, forgotten grave sites and large buildings which had, by the time he found them, fallen prey to the ceaseless encroachment of the dense forests."

"Eh?"

"They were *overgrown*, Desdemona. The jungle had almost completely covered the buildings and statues, with vines and ferns and all sorts of plant growth. Enormous trees had set their roots deep into the foundations of the walls and the floors, and many animals – monkeys and tigers, Lillian Bingal told us, orang-utans and other strange beings – now dwelled inside the partly ruined homes where once people had lived."

"Tigers?"

"Sumatran tigers."

Desdemona's feathers hackled, and she shivered with a jolt.

"Then, before I left to go to the Beauty Parlour and the Pyramids, Lillian Bingal told us of the Palace of Srivijaya, which is mentioned in that article from *Thoth's Blurter* upon which you have plonked your tarsus. She told us that Dr Schnitger had returned unexpectedly from his excavation of this site – the monsoon season had come early that year, and it was impossible for him and his team of excavationists to keep working in the rain and wind – and when she met him, Schnitger's eyes were wide, wider than she'd ever seen them. And I believe that she had probably seen his eyes wide on many an occasion, if you get my meaning..."

Desdemona sniggered, even though she didn't have a clue what he meant. Then she let her rough yellow tongue drop out from her beak, where it slurped up a coven of fleas from the underside of her pot-belly.

"According to Ms Bingal, Schnitger was incredibly excited at what he had found. She *hinted* in her lecture that it was the most amazing discovery that he had made ... little short of flabbergasting, going by the way she was describing it. But when one of the more eager students in the class asked her *exactly* what it was that Schnitger had found at the Palace – I believe it was that goody-goody Jim, now known as Jim of Cairo, who asked the question—"

At the sound of Jim's name, Desdemona's eyes throbbed harder than ever. "SCRAAAAAAARK! That waste of walking skills! Him and that gaudy, know-it-all macaw and that silent great humped beast of mange! Bleerrrrch!"

"For once, you and I agree on a topic. Arrr. Anyway, when Jim asked her for more details about the Palace, Ms Bingal would not say anything. She told us she had made a promise to Dr Schnitger not to tell, and there was nothing that would make her reveal any more about the Palace."

"Promises, promises, promises," repeated the raven, staring ahead.

"Well, when I remembered all of this, the first thing that shot into my lobes of Brilliance was to go and find Lillian Bingal and get the whole story out of her. Which is what I did when I tied you to the pillar with the sculpted head of Medusa in that underground water system in Istanbul—"

"M'feathers are still damp," she croaked. "And I still have nightmares about that big green face ... all them snakes ... eeeerggghhhhh."

"—and ventured to Cairo."

"Crark! So *that's* where you were for those five days."

"Arrr. Visiting Lillian Bingal at her home in down-town Zamalek."

"But how did you make her spill the beans? She'd made that promise, you said."

"So she had, so she had." Bone blew a shaft of smoke out the window, and his flabby lips curled into a smile. "I used one of my usual tactics: charming deceit."

"Eh?"

"I masqueraded as someone I was not."

"Not boldly disguised as Barbra Streisand again?"

"No, you scraggy sack of stupidity. I only did that once, in order to get those tickets to see the wrestling the year before last. No, I told Lillian Bingal that I was Gavin Schnitger, the son of Dr Schnitger, and that I had been away at sea for the last forty-two years."

"Gavin Schnitger?"

"Arrr. I thought it suited my understated swashbuckling persona. I have always liked the name Gavin."

"Sheesh! And she believed you?"

"Hook, line and Schnitger! It was easy, actually. I think the poor old dear misses Dr Schnitger so much that she was only too ready to believe such a story. Well, she invited me in for coffee and cake, and we talked. Oh, Desdemona, I sweet-talked her until I thought I was going to metamorphose into a lump of sugar. In no time at all she agreed to my request."

"Which was?"

"That I might be able to see any of my father's diaries or journals or any papers in which he had recorded exactly what he had discovered at the Palace of Srivijaya."

"Atta boy," rasped the bird, impressed with her companion's duplicity.

"And," Bone continued, his smile stretching wider beneath his beard and moustache, "I hit the nail right on the noggin. Dear old Lillian got up and hobbled over to an enormous bookcase – did I mention that she had only one leg? It doesn't matter, it's neither here nor there..."

"Well, where is it?"

"She – what?"

"Where is it?"

"Where is what?"

"Lillian Bingal's leg?"

"It's on her body, you idiot."

"No," she rasped, "not the leg she's still got, I mean the other leg."

"What?" A bead of impatient sweat popped out on Bone's forehead.

"Her other leg. The one she *hasn't* got any more. You said that it's neither here nor there. So where is it?"

"Well it must be in an altogether..." He stopped and rolled his eyes. "Oh, heavens to the goddess Betsy, why do I bother?"

"It seems strange if it's neither here nor there and she has ta go hobblin' all over the place, looking for it."

"ENSHUT YOUR BEAK! It was a figure of speech!"

"Screrk."

"Look, she went over to the bookcase and took out seventeen old, buckram-covered diaries, all of which had been written by Schnitger himself. She told me to look in the last one, which I did. There, in energetic and meticulous handwriting, as if a spider had skated across the pages with inky boots on, was all the information about the Palace of Srivijaya, and what Schnitger had found up there on top of the extinct volcano known as Gunung Dempo."

"What?" She turned to face him, her wings rising and falling with curiosity. "What'd he find? What are we gonna find?"

"Greatness," Bone answered enigmatically. "Arrrr. I speedily copied down the information into my black pocket-journal and, once it was done, I left the old woman alone with her memories."

"And her missing leg."

"Shut up."

From behind them, deep inside the back of the van, a low, solemn dirge started.

Bone raised his eyebrows. "What on earth is that?"

"Them women," scowled Desdemona. "They've been doin' that for the last three days. On and off. It took me a while to realise it, but they're singing."

"Singing?"

"Yep. They usually do it after you've served 'em that special Turkish tea with the Obsequious Pills in."

"I see." Bone shuddered – the sound of the song was melancholy and slow, and, being out here on the dark and deserted road, with the looming black shapes of trees and bushes all around, was beginning to make him feel decidedly creepy. (He had always believed that jungles and rainforests were places of great sinisterness, and should all be burned or ripped down to the bare earth.)

"Say," whined Desdemona. She jerked her wingtip in the direction of the Turkish women. "What've all of *them* got to do with this? Why do you need 'em?"

"You'll see when we get to the top of Gunung Dempo."

The dirge continued, flowing like a slow, swelling wave on a sad but calm lake, coming in and receding, onto the shore and back into the water:

> *"Oooh, oooh, oooh,*
> *olay, olay, olay,*
> *oooh, oooh, oooh,*
> *olay, olay, olay..."*

Desdemona stared at the silhouetted trees and the dark, desolate road. "They call that song 'The Cup of Life'," she croaked.

"Arrrr," sneered Neptune Bone. "Soon, very soon, my cup will be running over. Mark my words, Desdemona. Mark my words."

In the foothills at the base of Gunung Dempo, the crashed plane lay still and silent.

A soft wind blew through the grasses and trees. Somewhere far off, a lone fireback pheasant gave a long shriek – loud and shrill – that pierced the stillness of the night.

All afternoon and through the approaching twilight, there had been no movement from inside or outside the shattered aircraft. No animals had crept out of the jungles to prowl around it or to investigate what was inside. No sounds had come from within. The plane had remained where it had come to rest, tipped onto its side, dented and broken, its wheels ripped clear off from the undercarriage and its one remaining wing twisted and smashed, with the tip dangling limply, like a broken limb.

But now, as the evening was thickening, and the jungle settling down into its night-time activity of growing and scavenging and soaking up the moonshine, a faint, glowing light began to emerge from the upper part of the track that snaked down from the crater of Gunung Dempo.

It was a long cluster of light, and it appeared to be gliding, smoothly but a little slowly, as if it was filled with hesitancy.

It was very pale, very faint, almost as if it was composed of only the flimsiest of beams.

As it descended further, it started to leave the track, seeping into the semi-thick growth of trees and ferns and coarse bushes that separated the side of the volcano from the grasslands of the foothills.

Through the foliage the glowing cluster of light travelled, under the darkened boughs and branches and past the gnarled, shiny vines. Disturbing nothing as it went; everything was still; not even a lizard rustled through the leaves.

Soon the trail of glowing light came to the crash site.

And, as the glowing light settled, it began to reshape itself in some silent, careful way, as if the breeze were picking out sections of the glow and rearranging them into definite shapes.

Shapes that resembled human beings.

Very soon, this part of the forest was filled with pale, glowing figures that resembled human beings. But there was something about them that made them look *unlike* human beings as well...

Maybe it was the way the moonlight was filtering weakly through the trees, or maybe it was because of the shimmer that was coming from many of the leaves and clusters of fronds and the weaving, twisting, shiny vines, but it seemed that each of these pale, glowing, human-like figures did not have any clearly defined edge to it.

Each figure appeared to have faint features: eyes, noses, openings that looked like mouths. They all had a rough outline of legs and arms, but no more: where fingers and ears and the details of clothing should have been, there was only a faintness that dwindled out against the surrounding darkness.

Each of the figures was a shape, shimmering and present, yet not *quite* present as well.

Each shape was a patch of haze, surrounded by its paleness and the jungle.

Each shape remained motionless.

Each shape made no sound at all.

Each of them watched. Each saw the smashed plane against the ironwood tree.

Each of them seemed to be waiting.

The seconds crept by until they were minutes. The minutes became hours. The first morning birdsong, of a hundred different species, began to trill and spread through the treetops.

Soon the sun would come and gild everything, and a new day would commence.

More quickly than they had come, the pale, glowing figures joined into a group again. With not a sound or breeze or disturbance of the soft mulch on the forest floor, the group became a cluster. The cluster of light glided back from where it had come: towards the track that led up to the flat top of Gunung Dempo.

And still the plane was silent.

Part Two:

THE LIGHT AMONGST
THE TREES

◎ ◎ ◎ ◎ ◎ 9 ◎ ◎ ◎ ◎ ◎

THE DAMAGE DONE

THROUGH HER DUSTY EYELASHES, Brenda the Wonder Camel surveyed the damage around her.

Apart from a few bruises to the tops of her humps, which were wedged hard and tight against the ceiling of the plane, she was unhurt; when the plane had plummeted and rolled, she had been hurled across the interior of the cabin, and her carpet had been pulled from under her by the explosive force and tossed into the air.

A section of the seats in front of her had been torn out when the plane had smashed into the tree, and had become wedged endways in a big gash in the floor of the aircraft, pinioning Brenda firmly against the ceiling.

Try as she might, she was stuck fast. Her head and part of her neck protruded from behind the seats, and she could see the cockpit, half-inverted, at the end of the plane. It was so near, yet so far away, it may as well have been at the other side of the world.

When the sun had set and the jungle night had risen up to shroud the plane in the earthy-smelling darkness, all Brenda had heard had been silence. Not calm silence, or hopeful silence, or silence full of the promise of something about to happen, but flat silence. No noise of hinting.

 86

This silence had worried her immensely.

She had snorted at first: low snorts, questioning and scared, but there had been no answer from Jim, Doris or Jocelyn. Eventually the Wonder Camel had given up snorting and struggling to get out from behind the seats. She tried, instead, to glimpse her friends.

She tried and tried, craning her head as far as she could wide of the seats, but all she could see were these things: lots of broken glass; seats that were torn and dented; and, dimly, Jocelyn's sleeve and her hand, dangling motionless from the seat in which she was (Brenda hoped) still seat-belted; a tangle of still, unmoving feathers from under the seat where Cairo Jim had been sitting; and Jim's pith helmet, which had been hurled into the cabin of the plane, and which lay, with battered brim, on the side of the plane which was now the floor.

Then darkness had seeped into the ruined aircraft, and the night had stretched endlessly before her.

The sight of these things, devoid of movement, filled Brenda with a dread she had never known in her long Bactrian life.

Through the hole where the wing had been ripped clean away, the first faint shafts of morning light began to pour. Into the cabin they came, soundlessly, warmly, pale yellow shafts of sunshine that weaved upwards and downwards, back and forth, like golden fingers searching for something they could not find.

The shafts moved slowly across the wall–floor of the plane, creeping up over the wedged bank of seats, until, with no sound or fuss, they danced across Brenda's nostrils and lower snout.

Brenda had been dozing – a panic-laced half-slumber that she had fallen into because of her exhaustion and helplessness. As the sunlight tickled her nostrils, they twitched and flared.

"Ah-ah-ah-ah-quaaaaaaoooo!"

Her sneeze woke her, and her eyelids sprang open. She blinked heavily and watched the shafts of light moving – across her head and up, through the shattered cabin and towards the cockpit.

And then she heard a voice – a voice so welcome, so unexpected, so full of life, that Brenda's heart danced a tango-beat of exhilaration.

"Well, it's about time you surfaced! Methinks you've had enough beauty sleep to last you four lifetimes! Rark!"

There sat Doris, a few metres from Brenda's snout. The dusty bird was stretching her wings, raising them and lowering them, and shaking out her feathers.

"Doris, my sweet friend," Brenda thought with a great rush of Wonder Camel telepathy. *"How long have you been awake?"*

Doris blinked and looked at her. "I've only been awake for about a quarter of an hour or so," she prerked. "When we crashed I must've got flung under the seat there. Ouch. At least I'm not hurt, though.

 **88**

Just a bit of feather stress, but that'll pass."

"Quaaaooo?" snorted Brenda, peering past Doris and into the cockpit.

"Don't worry, Bren," said Doris, hop-fluttering up onto one of the seats that held Brenda. "Jim's gone outside with Jocelyn Osgood. I woke Jim first ... I feathered his face with some water from his water bottle. Took some doing, but at last he came around. He's all right, except for a big gash behind his ear and down his neck. Long, but not too deep. Luckily the blood had stopped flowing by the time I woke him. But we bandaged that and he's acting calmly."

"Quaaaaooo!"

"Methinks it'll heal soon enough, but our friend might have a bit of a scar down that side of his neck. Rark."

"And Jocelyn?" Brenda telepathised urgently.

"Jocelyn Osgood seems all right. I'd say the seat-belt saved her from too much damage."

"Can she see again?"

Doris picked up on Brenda's thought. "And she can see again, too. Must've been temporary blindness. Jim thinks she's broken her left thumb, and he's put a splint on it and wrapped it tightly. Apart from that, she's chirpy, if you'll pardon the expression."

Brenda fluttered her eyelashes and tried to squirm.

"Now you stay calm for a few more minutes, Brenda. Jim and Jocelyn Osgood are looking for a big branch or something to lever these seats away from you. Then we'll have you out in two shakes of a Wonder Camel's tail, you wait and see!"

Outside, Jim was dragging a long, sturdy branch back to the plane. He had half-broken, half-cut it from a nearby myrtle tree, using his small Fear Not the Obstacles of Time, Place or Rugged Jungly Places Archaeological Machete.

He found Jocelyn sitting on a rock, staring at her broken aircraft. From behind, he saw how her shoulders were slumped.

"Joss?" he said quietly, dropping the end of the branch behind her and putting his hand on her shoulder. She kept looking at the plane, her face turned away from him.

Gently she reached up and patted his fingers, being careful not to bump her splinted thumb.

"I'm really sorry about the plane." He spoke carefully, being as gentle as he could. "I know how much it meant to you. How long you've always wanted one of your very own."

Slowly she shook her head, her dusty auburn curls being blown by the small early-morning breeze.

"I know how hard you've saved for it and everything. You really deserved that plane, after all the Flight Attending you've done, and all the waiting on those passengers, and all the longings you've had to be a pilot yourself, in your very own aircraft and all."

She let go of his fingers and he saw her shoulders shaking a little.

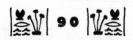

A big lump gathered in the archaeologist-poet's throat. He felt greatly responsible for what had happened, and dreadful that it had been he who had shattered her dream. "There was nothing I could do, Joss, nothing else. When Doris saw those huge boulders of hard lava at the end of the road—"

Her shoulders were heaving now.

"—I *had* to swerve round here. If I hadn't, I bet my bottom piastre that we'd all be—"

And there he stopped, as his ears were regaled with one of the most joyous sounds he knew:

Jocelyn Osgood threw back her head, looked up at him, and laughed – a mighty, relieved, tinkling laugh that ignited every pore of delight in Cairo Jim's body.

"You ... you've been laughing? I thought you were so upset, you..."

"Of course not, you lovely, dear man. Why should I cry?"

He came round and knelt in front of her, tilting back the brim of his pith helmet and looking into her vivid eyes. "You've lost your—"

"—big lump of steel and aluminium and glass and rubber bits? That's all it was, Jim. A thing. Far more important than that, *we're* all here. Aren't we? You, Doris, Brenda and me?"

His heart surged with a warmth that thrilled him. (It was a warmth he often had when Jocelyn made a lot of sense.)

"That's the most marvellous thing," she went on.

"I can replace *that*" – she waved her hand at the twisted, mangled wreckage – "any time I want. I can save my money again, and work more shifts, and serve more passengers. That's only a *thing*. I can't replace the friendship I have with you, or Doris, or Brenda."

He smiled at her.

"I'd hate to lose you, Jim of Cairo."

"And I you, Joss of the Skies." He felt his face redden, and was glad when Doris flew out from the hole in the side of the plane and came to perch on his shoulder.

"Rerark! Come on, you two. Brenda's been wedged against those seats so long she's starting to evolve into a lounge suite!"

Jim stood and picked up the branch. "Let's go and extricate our friend."

"And," said Jocelyn, scanning the track that rose up the side of Gunung Dempo, "see what it is that's brought us all here."

The branch was sturdy, and Jim was good at finding the correct angle and place to put it, so it was only five minutes before he had levered the seats out of the hole and away from the Wonder Camel.

With shaking, cramped legs, Brenda stood. Pausing only to snout Jim gratefully on the side of his arm, she went out of the shell of the plane and into the new day.

Doris began waddling through the mess inside the cabin, pulling out small belongings with her beak.

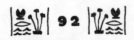

"Here's Jim's compass," she announced, finding it half-embedded in the soft, torn padding of the ceiling. "And Bren's Melodious Tex novel." That had been pushed hard against one of the unbroken windows, spread open and flattened, like some unnaturally compressed bird with its wings stretched wide.

Jocelyn collected the items when Doris found them, and placed them safely outside, where Brenda and Jim repacked the saddlebags and Jim's and Jocelyn's knapsacks.

The order of things began to return. Soon everything had been retrieved from the mess. Jim and Jocelyn saddled up Brenda, secured the bags to the sides of her saddle, and put their knapsacks on.

"How's the thumb, Joss?" asked Jim.

She moved her splinted thumb up and down. "Hurting less and less."

"Quaaaaooo," snorted Brenda, turning her head towards the track in the distance. The sun was high in the sky now, and everyone could see the way the leaves from the trees cast a dappled, shifting light onto the track as it threaded its way up the volcano.

"Let's go," said Cairo Jim, securing his knapsack's strap and taking hold of Brenda's bridle. He started to walk her towards the track.

"Too right," Doris screeched. She cast a final glance at the ruined plane, and clucked her beak. "We've survived that. Now nothing can stop us!"

⊚ ⊚ ⊚ ⊚ ⊚ **10** ⊚ ⊚ ⊚ ⊚ ⊚

ADDICTED TO GLOVES

"TEA'S UP, LADIES!"

On the other side of the Bukit Barisan mountains – the western side of Gunung Dempo – Neptune Bone flung open the rear doors of the pantechnicon. Behind him, on a small picnic table, sat the large copper samovar. Next to this were eight mugs of piping hot tea (laced with large amounts of Bone's exclusive Obsequious Pills), steaming and ready.

Out of the van tumbled the eight burly women. Fatimé Breeches rushed to Bone. "Where? Where is the tea, Mr Glamourdust? It has been such a long time between drinks!"

He extended his pudgy forefinger and swept his arm in the direction of the table. "Look no further, madam!"

All of the Turkish Women's Olympic Championship Tent Erection Team swooped upon the table and snatched up the mugs.

Bone watched as they gulped down the brew. "Such is the power of addiction," he said to Desdemona, perched on his shoulder.

"Not only that, but they can't get enough of it," she croaked.

Bone rolled his eyes.

 94

"So, chubbychops, what now? What're you gonna do with the Twoctet?"

He was in the act of swiping her from his shoulder, but his arm froze in mid air. "The Twoctet? What on earth is the Twoctet, you deluded Darwinian dropout?"

Her eyes throbbed at him. "The Twoctet," she repeated.

"Yes, yes, I heard you the first time. Enlighten me, Desdemona."

She puffed out her drab black chestfeathers. "If you take all the first letters of the Turkish Women's Olympic Championship Tent Erection Team, it makes Twoctet. It's what you humans call an *acrimony*."

"No, you miseducated mess of malice. You are what we humans call an acrimony. The Twoctet is what we humans call an *acronym*."

"Acrimony, acronym, whatsa diff? It's all just words anyway."

Bone raised his arm and finished swiping her away. "With your pathetic indifference to the written word, you should go into politics," he sneered.

She half-fell, half-fluttered into the air. "Nevermore, nevermore, nevermore. I prefer *undisguised* villainy, like what we're doin'."

"Arrrr."

"Please, Mr Glamourdust." Dënise had bounded up to his side, and was looking at him with big, devoted eyes. "What shall we do now for you?"

"Oh, for croakin' out loud!" said Desdemona.

"I'm glad you asked, Dënise," purred Bone, reading her name on the embroidered patch sewn onto her tracksuit top. "I need you and a few of the other women to go into the forest out there and cut me down two very long poles of hard wood. They must be strong enough to take my weight and the weight of my luggage and supplies. And collect some bamboo and fern fronds as well."

Dënise bit her lip, thinking. Then she slapped him – very hard – on his back. "Ah! I know what you are planning! Yes, I'll organise a small group."

Bone picked himself up off the grass (he had landed heavily on his knees, much to the delight of Desdemona, who laughed so much her feathers tingled). "Arrrr." He brushed off his plus-fours trousers fussily.

"Fatimé!" shouted Dënise. "Mr Glamourdust wants us to do a job for him. Kaynarca! Osmana! Fiona! Quickly!"

"You'll need this," said Bone. He went to the driver's compartment and took out, from under the seat, a long machete.

"CRAAAAAAAARK!" howled Desdemona. She flew like a bullet onto Bone's shoulder. "Ya mean ta say, you're gonna give 'em *that*? You trust 'em with a sharp instrument like that, after what you've done to 'em?"

"Never underestimate the power of addiction," he hissed back at her. "Dënise, take this machete and—"

"*I'll* take it, not Dënise." Fatimé stepped forward

and held out her hand. "That is, if you do not mind, Mr Glamourdust."

Bone frowned. He detected the faintest snarl of defiance in her tone.

"I am," continued Fatimé with throaty authority, "the Captain of this Team. It is how we always work: as a Team. And the Captain should always take charge." She thrust her hand closer to the machete.

Desdemona looked at Bone. He looked at Dënise.

"This is right," Dënise agreed, nodding solemnly. "Forgive me, Fatimé, I got carried away. I was so eager to help Mr Glamourdust in his plans that I forgot how things should always be done."

"That is all right, Dënise," said Fatimé. "Now, Mr Glamourdust, may I have the machete? Then I shall lead my Team to carry out your desires."

"Er…" a bead of sweat dribbled down from his forehead. "First, one question: have you drunk *all* of your tea?"

"Every last drop," answered Fatimé. "It is so delicious, Mr Glamourdust." She stared at him in an almost challenging manner.

"Show me your mug."

Fatimé fetched her mug from the table. She turned it upside down. "See? Nothing left."

Bone examined the mug carefully. He lowered his caterpillar-like eyebrows and looked sideways at Fatimé. "In that case, here." He handed the machete to her.

"Come, girls. Dënise, tell me what Mr Glamourdust needs us to get." Fatimé hitched up her tracksuit pants and led her women off into the deep green of the forest.

"Well, I'll be fondued," said Desdemona. "For a moment there, I thought we were goners!"

"Those Obsequious Pills truly are a marvel." Bone breathed a great sigh of relief and wiped his brow.

The raven flew from his shoulder and onto the table. "So, what're you gonna make 'em do with these poles they're fetchin'?"

"They will make a litter."

"A litter?"

"Arrr."

"What, like in trash and garbage?"

"No, you wretched wraith of wrongness. A litter to carry me and my luggage."

"Like I said, trash and garbage."

"Enshut yourself. They will attach some of the blankets I found in the back of the pantechnicon to the poles. And they shall build a canopy from bamboo and fern fronds. I shall lie comfortably on the blankets, shaded by the canopy, surrounded by my belongings, and the women shall carry the poles over their broad and strong shoulders. In this way, I shall be transported up the track."

"You really work it all out, don't you?"

"All part and parcel of being a Genius. Knowledge comes into it as well, you know."

"Knowledge?"

"Arrr. I happen to know that this track we are about to ascend is the quickest and safest way to get to the top of Gunung Dempo, where Dr Schnitger's Palace of Srivijaya should await us. I read about this track in his diaries, and made a note of it in my pocket-journal. Apparently, there's another track on the other side of this dormant volcano that is quite dangerous, and which takes much longer to climb."

"I see."

"But we should have no trouble at all, thanks to my ever-willing women and my brilliance of foresight. Now come, Desdemona, before the Twoctet returns – I have some itchy gunk embedded between my toes and I need you to get it out with that tongue of yours. Arrrr."

11

TO THE FLOOR OF HEAVEN

FOR NEARLY THREE HOURS Jim, Doris, Brenda and Jocelyn had been walking upwards.

The track ahead was a narrow, snaking ribbon of brown, twisting steeply along and up the side of Gunung Dempo.

The humidity and heat hung about them like an invisible, wet towel: heavy, clinging, and damp.

Brenda led the way, treading carefully yet purposefully on the hard earthen trail. Her flanks were glistening with a light coating of moisture, but, being a Wonder Camel, she was able to keep herself cooled through her unique, in-built Bactrian circulatory system, which acted as a natural air-conditioner. (She was accustomed to heat, but heat of a drier kind – the campsite in the Valley of the Kings was not known for its cool daytime temperatures.)

Sometimes Doris sat on the pommel of Brenda's saddle, keeping a watchful eye on the trail ahead. Now and then she would flex herself up and down, offering bits of advice to Brenda. "Mind, Bren, there's a big muddy bit there!" Or, "Careful of that pot-hole!" Or, "Have you ever thought about having an earring?" (Brenda snorted in the negative to that suggestion.)

Other times, the garrulous macaw would flutter back to Cairo Jim and descend onto his pith helmet or his shoulder. She would rub her beak up against the side of his clammy neck, making sure he wasn't overheating. If she thought he was getting too hot, she would squawk loudly that it was time for him to have a drink from his water bottle. The archaeologist-poet always did, whenever he was thus advised.

Jocelyn and Jim had started walking together, side by side, but soon Jocelyn had become intrigued by the beautiful vegetation growing on the side of the volcano. She had gradually slowed her pace, falling a little way behind the others, and let her eyes be filled with all the colour.

It had been a long time since she had been in a jungle, and she had almost forgotten the beauty of greenness. Almost forgotten that one single colour could have so many shades, so many different moods to it.

Here, on the steamy side of Gunung Dempo, there were giant palm fronds that radiated sharply outwards in the shape of fans. They were a luminous green; bright and light, as though they had caught the sun's rays and were keeping them prisoner within their fronds. Huge clusters of these fan-palms would appear along the track, and then there would be none for a few hundred metres. Then another cluster would cover the volcano side, dense and sharp and splayed wide, their spiky tips stretching towards the sunlight.

Occasionally the branches of an ancient, sweet-smelling sandalwood tree would overhang the track, drooping heavily, weighed down by smotherings of dark green vines.

Dotted about, between the fan-palms and the vines, were countless, tiny, gently feathery ferns. They sprang out of the side of the volcano in places where one would not have expected anything to be able to grow. These were Jocelyn's favourites of all the plants. They were perched there, sometimes at strange, bold little angles that almost defied gravity. These minuscule ferns were glowing-green, bright and proud amongst all the giants around them, as if they were saying, "Look at us! Look at us! We're alive and healthy too!"

It was these smallest of plants that reminded Jocelyn why she liked jungles and rainforests: no matter what the size, there was always room for any kind of plant. And, as she well knew, all the vegetation depended on whatever was around. The huge plants could not have survived without the smaller ones, and vice versa.

There was such a variety of trees growing along the edge of the track that sometimes Jocelyn found it hard to believe, even though she was seeing them with her own eyes, that they were all growing together in the one location. Not only were there the palms and the sandalwoods, but there were also stands of myrtles, clusters of chestnut trees – old, wizened and some of them rotting, ironwood and camphorwood, and dark-boughed ebony trees.

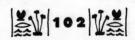

There were great, impenetrable walls of bamboo pressing hard against the side of the volcano, their stalks ranging from brownish-green all the way through to near-iridescent golden-green.

And then there were the flowers: thick, damp clumps of rhododendrons – pink, white, mauve – suddenly bursting forth amid the greenery. Or startling appearances of delicate, yellow-speckled orchids growing in mossy, unexpected and precarious places.

The sunlight shifted and dappled along the track, disappearing at times when the foliage blotted out the sky. At other times it would flicker across the leaves and vines and ferns and flowers, creating a mini-kaleidoscope of changing shades – bright and yellowy green, faint and greyish green, cobwebby silvery green, calm olive-green and bold, rich-as-Paradise green.

All of this abundance of verdant growth and beauty kept Jocelyn's mind off her ruined aircraft and her thumb, which was now only mildly painful.

As he walked, Jim's mind was buzzing with the anticipation of what lay ahead. Every step was a step closer to whatever it was. Maybe they would discover the secret of Schnitger's expedition. What *had* gone on at the Palace of Srivijaya that made the Palace and the grounds so amazing? Maybe they would discover nothing at all. Either way, the eagerness he always felt whenever he was pursuing another mystery of history filled every molecule of Jim's body.

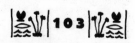

His shirt was dark with perspiration, and the top of his socks, poking out above his Sahara-boots, were ringed with a moist heat. He felt very warm, but very glad to be alive, here in this fresh, teeming-with-life, shimmering-with-uncertainty place.

The heat and anticipation intermingled, slowly and creepingly, with the unexplained things that had been somehow stored in his poetry cells. Very soon, as his pace continued, a verse was swirling about in his mind and, before he knew it, he was reciting, quietly and clearly:

"What draws us on to the unknown,
what makes us turn the unturned stone?
Why do we search for secrets lost,
into the winds of History tossed?
What drives us to uncertainty?
What makes you you? What makes me me?
Why—"

"Raaaaaark!" Doris flapped her wings tetchily. "I'd suggest you stop that one, Jim, before you give yourself a headache!"

Jim blinked and frowned. Maybe Doris was right... that sort of poem might be better to work on back at camp, when it was safer for his mind to wander.

On they climbed, the track gradually becoming steeper as the hours passed. Doris suddenly twitched between Brenda's ears.

"Raaaaaark," she raaaaaarked, slowly and softly, as if she had a small roll of thunder trapped in her throat.

Brenda stopped walking, aware that Doris could sense something in the air around them.

Cairo Jim stopped as well, and dabbed at his forehead with his handkerchief. "What is it, my dear? What's up?"

Her beak jerked to one side and then to the other. "Listen," she chirruped.

Jocelyn caught up with them. "Something wrong?" she asked when she saw the perplexity ruffling through Doris's feathers.

"Doris is sensing something," Jim told her.

"Oh." Jocelyn looked all around, and noticed how still everything had become.

"Not long now," Doris announced. Then she began a soft countdown: "Five, four, three, two, one..."

Almost as soon as she had said "one", a huge explosion of birdnoise shot up, into the skies: hundreds of thousands of birds, screeching and wailing and singing and laughing.

As the cacophony continued, Doris reeled off the sorts of birds she could hear, screeching over the noise to make herself heard: "Reeraaark! That's a firebird pheasant! And a squawking of little Malay parrots – cheeky birds! And listen – a flock of red-breasted bee-eaters! And – oh, upon my crest – it's a contest between some Sumatran woodpeckers and helmeted hornbills! Methinks the woodpeckers will win this one.

Talk about a racket! And there – an excited cackling of partridges!"

Brenda tried to flap her ears down to keep out all the commotion.

"I could sense this coming in m'feathers," squawked Doris above the barrage. "Every bird knows that this happens when rain's on the way."

"Rain?" Jim said. He took off his pith helmet and scratched his head. "But, my dear, the sky is as clear as a—"

"Oh, no it's not," thought Brenda. *"Look up there!"*

"Oh, no it's not," shouted Jocelyn. "Look up there!"

Above the pinnacle of Gunung Dempo, the sun was being squeezed out of sight by a fast-rolling battalion of heavy clouds, purple-black and bulging with great, swelling quantities of rainwater.

Doris blinked. "Told you so."

Jim knew tropical rainstorms from experience, and how heavily and quickly the rain would fall. On this track that could be dangerous. "It's going to burst," he yelled above the noise of the birds and the distant thunder that was echoing from nearby mountain tops. "Quick, let's take cover! Up ahead, see, there's an escarpment. We should all be able to fit under that rock until it passes over!"

"Well push me back and forth for a fortnight and call me a holding pattern!" blurted Jocelyn. "Look, everyone, up there!"

Shielding her eyes, the Flight Attendant was peering up to the sides of the flat crater that crowned Gunung Dempo. Jim, Doris and Brenda looked in that direction as well.

And they all saw something that sent a chill down their backs, feathers and humps.

As the sun was being swamped by the rolling mass of cloud, its last rays were needling down to the crater in thin, brilliant, utterly golden shafts. These shafts were moving frantically back and forth, faster and faster, as though they were great fingers playing a final, desperate concerto on the keys of some mountainous piano.

Quicker and quicker the shafts moved, spindlier and spindlier as the dark clouds all but obliterated the sun.

But, beautiful though the display was, this wasn't what made the four below gasp loudly.

Shooting upwards from the crater at the pinnacle of Gunung Dempo, like an answering echo, came dozens of bolts of brilliant, strong, yellow light.

And, as quickly as it had come, the cacophony of bird noise stopped, one two three!

"Well, swoggle me with a shimmer," whispered Cairo Jim. He took off his sun-spectacles and watched the bright and shifting display.

"That yellow light," said Jocelyn, still shielding her eyes, "is the same light I saw from above, just before I lost my sight!"

"Rark! Are you sure, Jocelyn Osgood?"

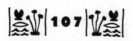

"No doubt about it. I'll never forget the lustre of that yellow ... it's brilliant almost beyond belief! I've never seen another yellow like it on all my travels!"

"Quaoooo!" snorted Brenda, as the clouds finally covered the last faint slither of the sun.

"Look!" cried Jim. "The yellow lights are disappearing!"

As the sky darkened almost entirely, the last vestiges of the yellow bolts of light from the crater-top dwindled and then faded, like a rainbow fades as the sun emerges. Only this time, no sun had emerged. Two seconds later, the clouds let loose their deliveries.

"Hurry!" shouted Jim. "The escarpment!"

The four of them raced to the overhang of rock as, all around them, great, fat drops of rain smashed and splashed onto the earthen track and the leaves and vines. The drops were so big and had such velocity behind them, they were like marbles being hurled from a great height; when they hit, they splattered into countless tepid droplets.

From underneath the small escarpment, Jim, Doris, Brenda and Jocelyn watched the downpour. Soon, the jungle was steaming: as the great drops hit the ground, big columns of mist broke out from the ridges and grooves the rain was making in the earth. These steamy shafts wove themselves all around the drenched trees and ferns, moving in and throughout the vegetation, shrouding some places thickly in their midst.

The sound of the rain deluging the volcano was like a relentless surging by some huge pack of elephants, moving forward through the jungle.

"That light," Jocelyn said. "It *was* the same as the light that blinded me. I'll wager my wings on it."

"What wings?" Doris asked with a slight trace of annoyance.

"My Valkyrian Airways Senior Flight Attendant Wings. The badge I wear on my uniform."

Doris merely blinked at the information – she had the real thing and didn't need a *badge* to fly.

"I wonder where that light comes from," said Jim, fanning his face with his pith helmet.

And whether it's anything to do with what Dr Schnitger discovered, thought Brenda, as the rainwater trickled down her mane and dripped in small pools onto the ground beneath her hoofs.

⊚ ⊚ ⊚ ⊚ ⊚ ⊚ **12** ⊚ ⊚ ⊚ ⊚ ⊚ ⊚

ASCENSION OF THE LITTER

THE TWOCTET HAD BUILT A FINE, sturdy litter out of bamboo, thick fern fronds, blankets and two indestructible lengths of teak poles, and all eight of the women were supporting this on their wide, muscly shoulders as they trudged carefully up the steep volcano path (which was not as steep as the track on the other side of Gunung Dempo).

Inside this vehicle, buffing his fingernails fastidiously with his antique fingernail buffer and occasionally popping a large, juicy grape into his flabby chasm of a mouth, rode Neptune Flannelbottom Bone. He had hoped that the canopy would protect him from being burnt by the sun's rays or bothered by annoying insects, but this plan had not been entirely successful: it was hotter beneath the canopy than outside it. Wide rivulets of perspiration seeped from his chubby cheeks and forehead, drenching his beard and dripping profusely onto his emerald-green waistcoat and paisley-swirled shirt.

The interior was cramped, not only because of Bone's fleshy body. Taking up space were his copper samovar and substantial Louis Vuitton Travelling Trunkette, and a big framed photograph of his

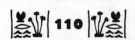

mother, Boadicea Tallulah Bone.

Desdemona perched on a knob of bamboo at the front of the litter, eyeballing Bone and the pathway ahead. She didn't bother asking him where he had obtained the grapes, even though she hadn't seen any growing along the jungle path. She knew that, underneath those massive contours of flesh and layers of wild, unbridled ambition, Bone was above all a Man of Means.

For hours now the women had hoisted their cargo up the wide path, grunting and huffing under the weight. Fatimé had instructed them to remove their lilac tracksuit tops before they had commenced the trek, and the women had tied their tops around their waists. Their dark blue T-shirts were now much, much darker and clinging to their mighty pectorals.

"Keep it steady, girls," grunted Fatimé, whenever one of them stumbled on a rock or into one of the many small ravines that lined the path. "Mr Glamourdust is precious to us all."

"Yes, Fatimé," would come the reply. "We would never want to cause him harm."

And all through their journey, the women thought about the next cup of delicious tea that Mr Glamourdust would soon serve them.

"Arrrr," sighed the fleshy man as he was rocked back and forth. "Just you wait, Desdemona, just you wait. When you see what I have found on *this* jaunt, you will be absolutely squawkless!"

"Yeah, yeah, and I'll be the President of Tashkent as well." She pecked at a flea on the back of her wing, and spat it savagely at the back of Dënise's head.

"I doubt that very much indeed, you moaning mutant monstrosity. You're about as useful to this world as a nose on a billiard ball."

She looked at him, her eyes throbbing hard as she tried to work out what he meant. Then she gave a small belch and turned to watch the path before them.

"You know," he purred, cramming seventeen grapes into his mouth and buffing his thumbnail as though it was a priceless artefact, "fhr tff fffst tmm nmm lerhhff, ehf mgrrfffl f fhhhloor."

"What in the Tower of Mabel are you talkin' about?"

With a loud gulp, he swallowed the grapes. "I said, for the first time in my life, I am grateful of failure."

"Well, that's a subject you could write an encyclopaedia about, isn't it? No one's failed in more highly public and spectacular ways than *you*, have they?"

He plucked a mouldy grape from the bunch and threw it at her skull. It splattered all over her headfeathers and slimed its way down towards her neck.

"You can do that until the cows come home, for all I care," she croaked. "You just obliterated at least two dozen fleas."

"Hmph. It is not *my* failure that I am referring to – or what you *see* as my failure – for I assure you that

I have not failed, I have just had one or two merely inconvenient setbacks along the path of life—"

"The day you were born was the biggest setback of them all!"

"Enshut that rancid beak, you excruciating excuse of entomophagous encumbrance!"

She glared at him, dizzy at his verbosity.

"No, the failure for which I am grateful is the failure of the Twoctet out there. Why, if they had not failed at the recent Olympic Games, I would never have been able to whisk them away to these tropical climes."

"Because they failed?"

"Because they failed. Arrrr."

"What's so special about the fact they failed? What difference would it've made if they'd *won*?"

"Oh, all the difference in the world, Desdemona. The main reason I took these women is because of their amazing and unsurpassed strength, which will be put to good use when we reach the crater of the volcano. But you see, I needed to get them away *secretively*, in such a way that they would not be missed."

"Eh? What's it got to do with 'em failing?"

"It's precisely because they failed that I have been able to carry out my plan. You see, we have just had the Olympic Games, have we not?"

She blinked and belched.

"And how long before the world has to endure these ridiculous spectacles again?"

"Um … another year?"

"No, foolish feathers, multiply that by four."

"Nine more years?" (Arithmetic had always been a great and deep mystery to the raven.)

Bone rolled his eyes and buffed with strokes of frustration. "Four years. Four whole years. One thousand four hundred and sixty-one days. Now that's a long time, Desdemona, a very long time. It's about the same amount of time since you last bathed."

"Mind yer own beeswax."

"So you see, it will be four years until the world will show any interest in these women again. They failed, miserably and hopelessly, and the world doesn't want to know about them. The fickle world will *forget* about them—at least until the next time they have a slight chance of being champions again."

"I see, I see, I see. The piastre's dropped! Because if they'd won, *everyone*'d want ta know 'em, eh?"

"Precisely. The eyes of the globe would be upon them. They'd be doing ads on the television for deodorants and sporting shoes and bananas and all sorts of things—"

"Like dishwashing liquid?"

"Yes, I suppose so, which is—"

"Lemon-scented dishwashing liquid?"

"Perhaps. Which is—"

"Lemon-scented dishwashing liquid that's gentle to the hands and doesn't make yer fingers go all pruney?"

"Yes, now will you—"

"And that can remove even the toughest grease and gunk and goo in practically no time at all?"

"Yes," Bone said through gritted teeth. "Which is—"

"I LOVE those ads. "Specially when that kid puts the bottle up to his nose and takes a big deep sniff. And then when he makes the cat sniff it as well. And then the canary. Boy, that's good advertisin', you can practically smell the—YAAARRWWOOOUUUGGGHHH!"

Bone had removed his shoe, and had hurled it swiftly through the litter, where it had made its presence felt against her belly.

"As I was trying to impress upon you, if the women had succeeded at the Olympics, they would be in demand. Everyone in Turkey, and possibly the rest of the world as well, would know what they were up to, and of their whereabouts. But now, because of their *un*success, they won't be missed. No one will be interested in them for a long time to come … except, perhaps, quite possibly in Australia, where sport is always of prime newsworthiness. Sporting events seem to be more important in *that* country than oxygen."

"Nevermore, nevermore, nevermore," moaned the raven, shuddering at the thought.

"So there you have it," said Bone. "A further tiny insight into my Plan of Boldness and Foresight."

"I've gotta hand it ta ya, my Captain. You think of everything!"

"Naturally." He peered out through a slat in the bamboo, up into the sky on the other side of the volcano. "Hmmm. Looks like there's quite a storm bucketing down over there on the eastern side. Those clouds are heavy. Lucky for us there's a wind blowing them towards the ocean. Rain is the last thing I need."

"I thought *I* was the last thing you need." She started to hop-flutter out of the canopy, towards Kaynarca at the side of the litter.

"Where are you going?"

"To do a little auditioning. See ya later!"

Bone sat back on his mattress of leaves and fronds and listened as, for the next hour, Desdemona hopped from one Turkish woman to the next, demanding that each of them recite "Gentler on your hands than a truckload of lemons, and kinder to your dishes than sunshine itself!" over and over and over.

It was late in the afternoon that the downpour stopped, just as suddenly as it had started.

"It's as if somebody up above turned off a tap quickly," said Jocelyn, peering up at the steamy side of Gunung Dempo and at the thick rivulets of water running down the track.

"Tropical rainstorms," said Jim, stepping out from the overhang of rock. "Like no other."

"We, of course," Doris crowed, "are somewhat used to them. Aren't we, Jim?"

"That we are, my dear. That we are."

Brenda stepped out onto the boggy track, and the swirshling mud rose up over the tops of her hooves. "Quaaaooo!" she snorted with some distaste.

All around, thick shafts of mist were rising, dancing

silently around the trees and vines and bamboos, before they dwindled away into the moist air.

Jim looked up at the sky, and at the top of Gunung Dempo. "The clouds have gone, so that's a good thing. I doubt we'll be getting any more rain today."

"Rark, glad to hear it. I'm so damp I feel like a feathered dishmop."

"But it'll be getting dark soon ... that sun is fast disappearing over the crater. I don't think we should continue until the morning."

"Shall we camp here, Jim?" Jocelyn said doubtfully, looking down at the mud beneath her feet.

"No, not here," thought Brenda, her Wonder Camel powers of observation coming to the fore. *"Look, ahead about five hundred metres."*

"No, not here," said Jim, "Look, ahead about five hundred metres. There's a place where the track widens. It's a clearing, I think."

Doris craned her neck. "It sure is! Let's go!"

They sloshed through the mud and up towards the place Brenda had spotted.

It was a semi-circular clearing – not very big, but not as muddy as the track, and there was enough space to pitch the two Presto! Toss It and It's Up in Six Blinks! Compact Tents, and to unfurl Brenda's Home-Away-From-Home Inflatable Camel-Comforter.

The clearing was bordered at the back, hard against the side of the volcano, by eight large camphorwood trees, whose branches formed a leafy canopy over the clearing.

"Just the place," Jim announced, slinging off his knapsack and helping Brenda with her saddlebags and saddle. "We'll see the night out here. Hopefully some of that rainwater flowing down from the top of the volcano will bypass us, and our trek might be a bit drier in the morning."

Everyone agreed it was a very sound suggestion.

Later, after the tents had sprung open and Brenda's comforter had been inflated, and a strong, narrow branch had been cut from one of the camphorwood trees to become a makeshift overnight perch for Doris, and when everyone had eaten dinner (tinned fruit for Jim, Jocelyn and Brenda and snails for Doris) and had settled down for the night, Cairo Jim woke with a start.

"Doris?" he whispered. He rolled over and pushed back the flap of his tent. "My dear, what's wrong?"

He wasn't sure how he had known that something was troubling the macaw – he had been in a deep and well-deserved sleep – but somehow he did know, and he had woken up.

The beautiful gold-and-blue bird was agitated, all right: there she was, pacing back and forth with tiny, waddling steps outside Jim's tent.

"What's the matter?" asked Jim.

"Couldn't sleep," she prowked. "I kept seeing the mists out there … coming up from below. They're *strange*, Jim. I've never seen anything like them, not in any jungles anywhere!"

118

"Why are they strange?"

"The shapes they make. Weird, the way they clump up like that. And the way they move. They seem to have some inner kind of light – almost as if they're lit up from within. Look, down there by those orchids. See?"

Jim scrunched his eyes and looked into the gloomy, warm night.

"Most patches of mist just hover for a while, hardly moving at all," said Doris. "But these misty bits of Gunung Dempo seem to move all about. Backwards and forwards."

All Jim could see was a faint patch of mist, unmoving and vaporous.

"As if they had some sort of purpose. Almost as if they're … they're *watching* us."

Jim shivered. "I think you're tired, my dear." He reached out and tousled her crestfeathers. "It's been an arduous trip so far. Maybe you're imagining a bit more than what you're actually seeing."

She puffed out her chestfeathers. "You wouldn't say that if it were Jocelyn Osgood making these observations."

He moved his fingers down until they were stroking the short, sharpish feathers at the sides of her beak – an action that Doris loved almost more than being a macaw. "Doris, my noblest and sweetest friend, you know that's not true."

She blushed beneath her feathers and gave him a playful nibble on the index finger. "I suppose so," she answered, her small eyes alive and bright with his affection.

"Now try and sleep. You'll be giving me nightmares with any more of this talk."

She turned her head once more to look at the misty shapes. "'Be not afeared'," she quoted,

"'the isle is full of noises,
Sounds and sweet airs, that give delight,
and hurt not.
Sometimes a thousand twangling instruments
Will hum about mine ears; and sometimes voices,
That, if I then had waked after long sleep,
Will make me sleep again; and then, in dreaming,
The clouds methought would open and show riches
Ready to drop upon me; that, when I waked,
I cried to dream again.'

"Rerark!"

When she had finished, Jim could see her little heart beating rapidly under her feathers. "Was that from Mr Shakespeare's *The Tempest*, by any chance?" he asked her.

"Spot on, buddy-boy." The feathers at the edge of her beak crinkled. "Who else?"

"Good night, my clever friend."

"Good night, my clever friend."

DAY OF DISCOVERIES

WITH THE SWIFT APPROACH of the jungle night, Bone had likewise decided to make camp, on the other side of Gunung Dempo.

He ordered the Twoctet to build a platform out of bamboo, upon which he (inside his litter) could be elevated above the mud and any crawling or slithering things that might decide to pay him any unwelcome visits. Three of the women – Osmana, Kaynarca and another named Bernica, who bore an amazing resemblance to an uncut block of granite with a curly wig on top – took to the task with great enthusiasm. They hacked down enough bamboo to build a platform four metres high and the same distance wide.

Throughout their hacking and building activity, Desdemona watched from the top of a rubber tree, silently, her eyes throbbing redder and redder as the night grew darker and darker …

Soon the Twoctet had carefully placed Bone inside his litter on top of the platform. He emerged briefly to serve them his special tea, which Desdemona lowered in the samovar to the ground. Then, when the women went off to build themselves makeshift huts, Bone crawled back into the litter and tried to make himself comfortable.

He had a stub of candle which he lit and placed on a small ledge in the bamboo wall. With a great deal of squirming of his fleshy limbs, he pulled out his black journal from the back pocket of his plus-fours. This he opened to the pages where he had jotted down the information he had gleaned from Schnitger's diaries, thanks to the unknowing help of Lillian Bingal.

"Arrrrr."

He groped around and found his cigar case. Still reading through the journal, he bit the end off a Belch of Brouhaha, spat it through the opening of the litter, and lit the cigar with his silver cigar-lighter.

He exhaled his first mouthful of the heavy, reeking smoke. And he froze.

There was something outside!

He stayed absolutely still, waiting to hear the noise again. It had been a *whoop-whoop-whoop* sound. Low and thumping, but not thumping against anything hard. Something huge was beating the air.

Fat beads of sweat formed quickly on his forehead. They ran down through his caterpillararian eyebrows and over his cheeks, where they became caught in his tangled beard.

His eyes moved to the left and back to the right.

Whoop-whoop-whoop! Again it came, louder than before.

His cigar was trembling in his pudgy fingers.

With a quavering voice, he called tentatively: "Fatimé? Dënise? Osmana?"

No answer.

"Heavens to the Goddess Betsy, is anybody there?"

WHHOOOP-WHHHOOOOP-WHHHHOOOOOP!

So close now it made the litter shudder!

"N-n-noooooo!" Bone wailed, his voice a small stream of sound almost strangulated by his terror. He had visions – crashing through his imagination – of all his past deeds returning to catch him, in one foulish swoop, coming in a great explosion of retribution for all of the things he had done to the innocent and the—

"Crark! Whatsa problem, chubby-chops?"

Bone swallowed and glared at the raven. "Y-y-you?" he stammered, his lip quivering uncontrollably.

"Well, it ain't Mother Teresa," croaked Desdemona.

"That sound ... the beating through the air ... that was *you*?"

"What a genius you are, to work that out." She pecked at a cartel of fleas on her inner thigh, and spat them out onto the platform.

"But it was so loud, Desdemona. So much louder than you normally sound."

She belched and started making herself comfortable on the blankets. "Must be the volcano. It probably makes noises sound louder than they normally do."

"You're saying noises become *accentuated*."

"If you want me to: Murst be ze volcarno. It prerbably makes noirzez zound loader zan zey noamally der."

He looked at her as though she had finally given up any claim on sanity.

"That was my French accent," she sighed. "With

a little bit of German and Spanish thrown in for good measure."

"You cretinous crater of cruddiness. Oh, why do I bother?" He put his pocket-journal away again and took a long, reassuring drag on the cigar. His companion's idiocy had restored his sense of superiority, and he felt more sure of things again.

"So, my Captain, I have one question."

"Arrr?"

"Are we nearly there yet?"

"Oh, yes, we are. We are very close to our glory. At sun's first light, we shall leave and continue. And, if I'm close to the mark – which I indubitably am – we should come across the Palace of Srivijaya sometime mid-morning."

"Good, because I'm gettin'—"

"*RWWWWOOOOOOOAOAOAAAARRRRRRR!*"

The roars from a pair of tigers, somewhere below but not far away, ripped through the night.

OOOHHH-HHHAAAAA-OOOOOOHHH-AAAA-OOOOOHHHH-HHHHAAAAAAA-ARKKKKKKK!

A family of flying lemurs took to the trees at the disturbance.

KKOOOKKOKKOKOKOOOOOOKKKOOOOOO!

A pack of tree shrews made their feelings known even louder.

"Oh, the sinisterness, the sinisterness!" wailed Bone, rolling quickly over and burying his face in the blankets beneath him.

★   ★   ★

Next morning, Cairo Jim stepped out of his tent and into a world washed clean and glistening by the rains of yesterday.

Everything seemed as fresh as the day it was first created. The leaves and fronds were shining with moisture; the smaller ferns close to the ground were dripping with the pure remnants of the downpour. The earth had dried out a little, and smelled damp and rich as the heat started warming it for another day.

Before long, Doris had woken (she had managed to get some sleep, but it had taken a while before she could put the notions of the misty shapes out of her mind) and was helping him pack up his tent, gathering the ropes tidily into small bundles.

There was a clop-clop-squelch-clop, and Brenda emerged through some gigantic ferns. "Quaaaaooo!"

"Morning, my lovely," Jim greeted her.

"Beautiful day," she thought with a flutter of her eyelashes.

"Beautiful day," Doris squawked.

"Anyone seen Joss?" asked Jim. Her tent was down and already packed into its small bag, which sat next to her knapsack at the rear of the clearing.

"Here I am," came her cool, confident tone from the greenery. She stepped through some bamboo, her hair wet and recently combed, carrying a bundle tied in one of her scarves.

"Rark. Found a shower, did we?"

"No, Doris, but the next best thing. There's a spring in there, just behind the trees at the back of the clearing. The water must flow straight out of the volcano. It's as pure as can be, and – would you believe it – not ice cold."

"No?" said Jim.

"Quaaoo?"

"Really?" Doris blinked.

"Really." She dumped the bundle onto the ground. "Most springs are icy cold, aren't they? But this water is almost warm."

"Hmmm," hmmmed Jim.

"What's in the scarf, Jocelyn Osgood? Yesterday's socks?"

"No, breakfast!" She crouched down and spread open the scarf, to reveal several bunches of miniature bananas, some plump figs, a dozen small things that looked like peaches, and handfuls of peanuts. "I found them all growing near the spring."

Jim smiled. "Should keep us going for a while. Energy food. Just what we need for today." He looked up at the steepness of the track that rose before them. "I think it'll be a bit tougher from now on."

Jocelyn smiled back. "Well, the tough will get going with gusto, won't they?"

"Rark!" Doris blinked, and her feathers tingled with surprise as she found herself agreeing with Jocelyn's sentiment exactly.

Jim had been right: today, things were tougher.

The track was much, much steeper than it had been yesterday. Sometimes it was like climbing stairs, up and up, always rising. The moist, wet-towel air clung to their clothing and feathers and Wonder Camel hair, and the sweat trickled constantly. Soon Jim's and Jocelyn's shirts were dark and damp, and sticking clammily to their skin.

Every half hour or so there would be a flattish place where the group could rest, and they were grateful for such places: they would sit (or, in Doris's case, perch) and let their calf muscles relax for fifteen minutes or so, replenishing their water supply whenever they came across another mountain spring.

Then, when they were slightly rested, they would start again, up and up the staircase-like slope of caked, muddy earth. They were soon to find out that these were the easy sections of the track.

Three hours later, the incline changed dramatically. They came to a place where the track narrowed to less than half the width it had been. And the staircase-slope steepened so much that to look up it, Cairo Jim had to crane his head so far back, the front of his neck became almost an extension of his chest.

"Nearly perpendicular in some parts, wouldn't you say?"

Doris was glad she had her wings; to have to walk up this incline with her tiny legs would take forever.

"Looks like it's single file for the rest of the way," Jim said. "Take it carefully, Brenda, my lovely – you might have to breathe in and contract your sides at some places."

"Quaoooo!" She fluttered her eyelashes in a don't-you-worry-I've-faced-worse-obstacles-than-this fashion.

And on, and upwards, the foursome trudged.

Late in the morning, after constant climbing and frequent resting, and more steady trudging (not to mention a good deal of fluttering and perching and watchful observations from Doris), they came to a sight that made them stop and gasp.

After a long, particularly narrow curve, the track widened for a short distance – no more than a hundred metres or so. The side of Gunung Dempo jutted out, hard and sheer, forming a deep ledge that ran along the wider section of track.

Growing on this ledge, dense and mighty, were the biggest flowers that Jim, Doris, Brenda or Jocelyn had ever seen!

"Well swoggle me with a stamen!" gasped Cairo Jim.

"Rark! What ever are they?"

"Put me on standby!" whispered Jocelyn.

There must have been at least three dozen of these orange, yellow and purply-red-flecked flowers jostling for position along the ledge. Each flower was nearly two metres wide and one-and-a-half metres high, and made up of five thick, fleshy petals. At the centre of each flower was a deep cup, which also appeared to be thick and fleshy.

"The petals look just like your human ear lobes," remarked Doris, "only much bigger. And better decorated."

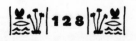

"What on earth are they?" said Jocelyn, more to herself than to the others.

Brenda the Wonder Camel flicked her tail, as the answer came filtering into her quiet, knowing mind. (When, as a young and inquisitive calf, she had accidentally eaten all twenty-seven volumes of the *Encyclopaedia Britannica*, she had gained a vast insight into much that was in the world, and all the information contained within those books had remained in her Wonder Camel system.) *"It's the* Rafflesia gargantua indestructibilia," she thought calmly and proudly.

"It's the *Rafflesia gargantua indestructibilia*," said Jim, removing his pith helmet and scratching his head.

"Really?" said Jocelyn.

"Tell us more," Doris urged him.

"Well, I don't know if there's any more I can…"

Brenda shook her tail, and sent out more information into Jim's receptive brain.

"I know," he continued with a start, "they're related to the order of flowering plants known as the Rafflesiaceae, named after the famous explorer of these regions, Stamford Raffles. The ordinary *Rafflesia* flowers grow to about one metre across, but these flowers before us – the *Rafflesia gargantua indestructibilia* – are the biggest of the species and are only found on the upper reaches of Gunung Dempo."

"Then we must be almost at the top," screeched Doris.

"What else, Jim?" asked Jocelyn.

Brenda wiggled her tail once more.

"Oh, yes." Jim put his pith helmet back on. "They're also the strongest flowers ever discovered on the planet, and their central cups and lobe-petals can withstand incredible heat and icy conditions. In fact, scientists have yet to find a way of destroying one of them."

"Remarkable." Jocelyn swigged some water from her water bottle.

"The only truly vulnerable part," Jim continued, "of such a flower is its stem."

"I'm after a closer look," said Doris. She raised her wings and flew to the closest flower, where she hovered and peered down into the cup. "Yergh," she said, screwing up her beak.

"What is it?" asked Jim.

"A baby orang-utan. At least, it *was* a baby orang-utan, once upon a time. It's been preserved in some sort of dark blue liquid ... yergh!"

Brenda's tail twirled, and Jim told them something more.

"Inside the cups of *Rafflesia gargantua indestructibilia* there are contained sacs of a lethal acid which kills any parasites or predators that get trapped within. This acid, known as 'indestructibilia juice', is only secreted whenever the moon is full. Prey is trapped within the cup of the flower until such times, when the indestructibilia juice is released. If the prey has not died of suffocation already, the indestructibilia juice will drown it and break it down so that the *Rafflesia gargantua indestructibilia* can digest it."

Jocelyn shuddered. "Danger-OUS!"

Doris hovered lower, until she was close to one of the lobe-petals. Accidentally, her wingtip brushed against the cool flesh of the flower.

"REEEEERAAAAARK!"

The lobe lunged upwards, as did all the other four lobes with a loud *ffffllluuubbbbb*. Doris shot out of the way with hardly a second to spare.

She flew back to Jim's shoulder as the flower closed up completely, and a dreadful smell of rotting vegetation – dead rodents, decaying leaves, putrefying waste and other sweet-sickening smells – filled the air.

"Time to move on," Jim said, clamping his handkerchief quickly across his mouth and nostrils.

"Jim," said Jocelyn, as one by one they walked carefully along the ledge and past the flowers, "how did you know all that stuff about the *Rafflesia gargantua indestructibilia* and the indestructibilia juice?"

The archaeologist-poet blinked behind his sun-spectacles. "Er ... um ... I guess it must've been something I once read."

"Quaaaaoo," snorted Brenda, letting her tail relax as she continued up the muddy track.

LET GLORY BE MINE!

THE HEART OF CAIRO JIM BEAT on with a growing, compounding rhythm as he and his friends rose higher on the narrow, winding track, and his mind kept turning over the same words as the heat and the steam increased:

> "Srivijaya, Srivijaya,
> will we find your legacy?
> Srivijaya, Srivijaya,
> is it lost to Eternity?
> Srivijaya, Srivijaya,
> has the jungle claimed it back?
> Srivijaya, Srivijaya,
> as we climb this epic track…"

On and on the beat kept going, as each footstep, hoofstep and beating of wings seemed to take more effort than the last.

That afternoon, like an overblown beetle bumping erratically along, the litter of Neptune Flannelbottom Bone, also known as Mr Preston Glamourdust, was nearing its destination – the Palace of Srivijaya.

"Arrr," he moaned, straightening his fez and trying not to crash too violently against the insides of his carriage and the samovar and his substantial Louis Vuitton Travelling Trunkette. "Be careful, ladies! Why has it got so rough all of a sudden?"

"Because, Mr Glamourdust," came Fatimé's throaty reply, "we are almost at the top. The path finishes in a few metres."

Bone's eyes lit up excitedly. "Did you hear that, Desdemona? We're here!"

"Crark." She pecked a gaggle of fleas from herself and tried not to sound too impressed.

"I think, that for the last few metres or so, I shall walk the rest of the journey."

"Oh, how magnanimous of you."

"Yes, but a bit of that sort of thing never goes astray, I always think. It'll set a good example to the Twoctet as well – they won't think that they're the only ones who've had to trek on this journey."

"You're so lazy you've gotta have a sleep before you can sneeze," muttered the raven under her rancid, seaweedy breath.

"Erf ... move out of the way before you get mussed by my presence." He slid and wriggled his body to the end of the bamboo platform and, in a voice which he imagined was reminiscent of Hannibal ordering his elephants to stop, he commanded the women to place – to *gently* place – the litter upon the path.

With a big chorus of (respectful) grunting, the Turkish

women lowered the contraption, placing it ceremoniously on the sloping dirt.

"Ooof, let me turn around … erfff … ouch, my tassel is caught on a splinter up there – Desdemona, come and help me with this fez!"

She hop-fluttered onto his shoulder and yanked the fez's tassel. There was a ripping noise, and the fez was freed.

"You stupid sap," he growled, looking at the torn strands of tassel embedded into the bamboo. "You can pay for that out of your wages."

"What wages?" she croaked, her eyes throbbing derisively. "You've never paid me a brass kazoo! What are the wages of sin anyway? Nevermore, nevermore, nevermore!"

"Enshut your beak and come with me." He slid his enormous, double-watermelon bottom along the floor of the litter and uttered a sharp squeal. "Yeouch!"

"What's wrong? Has your grandeur been tarnished?"

"Ooh! A splinter, right up my—"

"Well I'm not going anywhere near *that*! I'd never be seen alive again!" She raised her wings and shot out of the litter, coming to perch on a big, overgrown boulder at the side of the path.

"Wretched twerp," he said, wincing with discomfort. He thrust his legs out of the litter and placed his spats carefully onto the path. Then, in an act of greatness rising to meet the sun, he stood and surveyed the vista ahead.

"See?" said Fatimé, catching her breath and wiping her hot, moist forehead. "There is a wall ahead."

"So there is." His heart started beating a little faster, and he forgot all about the splinter. "The outer wall that fortifies the grounds of the Palace of Srivijaya. Arrr, Schnitger wrote of this very wall in his diaries!"

The wall was about two metres high, and in many places it had crumbled almost to nothing. It would not be hard to step over the mounds of rubble and into the Palace grounds. At various intervals along what remained of the wall, the jungle had started to reclaim the masonry, and thick, green, knotted vines had threaded themselves through weaknesses in the wall's joinery.

"Please, Mr Glamourdust," moaned Bernica. "It is hot and we are thirsty."

"Yes," agreed Osmana. "May we have some more of your special tea?"

"Please?" implored Dënise, wiping the streams of perspiration from her armpits with her tracksuit top, which she had untied from her waist for the very purpose.

"Just one cup?" beseeched Kaynarca, her thick eyebrows raised imploringly at him.

All the other women of the Twoctet raised their eyebrows similarly.

"Mm? Tea? Oh, arrr, of course." He snapped his chubby forefinger and thumb. "Desdemona! Hop into the litter and get the samovar and the special tea ready for the women." He popped two Obsequious Pills from a tube he kept in his waistcoat pocket and gave them to the raven.

"Put these into the samovar during the brewing process. When the tea is ready, the women may have two cups each, on account of their efforts in getting me this far."

"Two?" she asked him warily, slightly confused about the number.

"Arrr. They will need extra energy and verve for the task that is to befall them tonight."

"Tea! Tea!" chanted Dënise rapturously. "I saw a spring not very far back – warm water gushing from the mountainside. Give me the samovar, Mr Glamourdust, I will run back and fill it."

"You heard her, Desdemona."

The raven rolled her eyeballs and went into the litter. A minute later she emerged, tailfeathers first, dragging the huge copper samovar. "Here," she rasped.

Dënise grabbed the vessel and ran down the path, the perspiration flying off her enormous frame in all directions.

"And now to my destiny," Bone purred, his spine tingling with the unspeakable opportunity he would be able to confront tonight. "You may follow me, Desdemona, when the women have supped. Now I am going to enter the grounds of the Palace of the Maharaja of Srivijaya. Arrrrrr."

He lit a Belch of Brouhaha and off he sauntered, blowing foul columns of smoke into the steamy air.

Doris was riding on Jim's shoulder (she had varied her mode of travelling, sometimes flying and perching while she waited for the others to catch up, sometimes sitting on the pommel of Brenda's saddle, occasionally alighting on her best human friend as she was now doing).

As Jim trudged slowly and purposefully up the track, the macaw's mind was filling with the mystery of the Palace. What was it, she wondered, that went on there that made the place so special? Was it something about the Palace itself?

She gave a small *prrrrowk* as she let her imagination fill out her curiosity. Maybe the Palace of Srivijaya was made of a building material unlike that of any other monument? Maybe that's what made it so special, and this had something to do with why Dr Schnitger had been so unwilling to tell more?

But what could it have been, this strange building material?

Maybe, she thought, moving her neck up and down speedily, the Palace was built entirely of *glass*?

Perhaps (the feathers of her wings ruffled at this) it was carved out of *pure jade*?

Or (and she almost fell off Jim's shoulder when this conjecture came) it might have been made from something so absolutely and breathtakingly startling, something never before used in the history of architecture, that everyone who beheld it was instantaneously struck speechless?

And here her feathers really ruffled so much that it was like she had a small jiggling machine inside her instead of her skeleton:

What if the Palace of Srivijaya had been constructed entirely of egg shells?

Beautiful, opalescent egg shells from some special mountain bird – shells of the highest fragility and studded with rainbow-swirls of colour and speckles bright and sparkling?

"Cooooooooooooo," she cooooooooooooooed quietly at the thought.

"Steady on, my dear," said Jim, reaching up and stroking her tailfeathers (which were slapping against his back as though he was a door and they were a fist knocking for attention). "You'll have me going all jiggly as well if you don't settle down. The last time that happened I almost chipped a tooth, remember?"

"Rark, my apologies." She tried to steady herself and her ever-darting imagination, and concentrated on the track ahead.

Soon the Twoctet had finished their six cups of tea each (Desdemona had struggled with the concept of *two*, but had finally given up) and, picking up the Bone-less litter, they had followed their saviour and most adored man in the world into the ruins of the grounds of the Palace of Srivijaya.

Bone was relaxing on a paved courtyard terrace that had a view of the entire grounds. He had found himself a shady, cool spot beneath an ancient, sprawling fig tree. The tree's massive roots had long ago buckled and cracked the paving stones, and its trunk was the same thickness, colour and texture as the body of a mature elephant.

"Crark!" Desdemona flew to join him as he puffed on his cigar. "You don't look out of place there one little bit. Matter of fact, you blend right in."

"We have arrived, my frightful frustration of foolishness. Here at last, here where the marvels took place in the year 683. And where the marvels will come to their conclusion, under my illustrious hand, very soon. Arrrr."

She rolled her eyes at his grandness, and then hopped up onto a branch of the fig tree. From this vantage point she surveyed the scene above, below and around.

Great, twisting tree brances had spread overhead. The thick, leafy boughs had crept through the centuries, slowly, silently, ever onwards, until they had formed a dense, natural roof that covered all of what had been built in the grounds of the Palace of Srivijaya.

The only place not covered by this roof of greenery was in the centre of the compound. Here, the sunshine streamed down through a huge hole in the canopy.

The Turkish women had deposited the litter inside the Palace grounds, and they were all busy, their biceps and triceps awash with sweat, as they pulled and snapped bamboo poles from the thick clusters growing all around the site. In some places, the bamboo thickets were so well established that it was extremely difficult to see any traces of wall or anything else behind them.

"Crark. What's the Twoctet up to?"

Bone looked at Fatimé wielding the machete with terrifying force against one of the bamboo clumps. "I dare say they are doing as I ordered, and are making shelters for the night."

"We're stayin' the night here?"

"Oh, yes indeedy. We must, Desdemona. My whole Plan depends on it."

"What about them tigers that you told me about? Don't they live up here?"

"Perhaps." He flicked his ash at her. There was a loud sizzzzzzling, and dozens of fleas abandoned the singed bird.

"Thank you," she croaked.

"But I don't think you need to worry about tigers here. Why, look at all the strength and muscle-power of those eight creatures below. If any tigers dared to show their fangs here, the combined efforts of the Twoctet would soon put them to flight."

"Can Sumatran tigers *fly*?"

"No, you illiterate ignoramus of ignominity. It's a figure of speech."

"I knew that."

Desdemona turned, and her eyeballs throbbed redly as she scanned the grounds. She watched the women toiling in the heat, and her hatred of all women human beings swelled inside her, making her shudder violently and her fleas bite her more fiercely.

She saw the many small shafts of steam rising

silently from the cracks in the faded courtyard tiles.

After two minutes, she turned back to Bone. "What a waste of time!"

"I beg your pardon?"

"What a confounded and stupid waste of time it was comin' up here!"

He stared at her as though she were the worst smell in the world (to him, she was not far off such a state).

"I mean ta croak, why in the name of Tensing Norway didja make us come all the way up this stupid ex-stinked volcano? With all them ruffian sporting personalities? There's nothin' here but weeds and crumbled walls and vines and them eight Turkish women who think the sun shines outta your—"

"Arrrr, said enough?"

"No, I'm only gettin' started."

"You can complain until you're blue in the feathers, Desdemona. I do not care. Once again you have underestimated my foresight and dazzling ingenuity."

"Go on then. Tell me. What makes this dump so special to you and to us and to the future of our world?"

He stood, his fatty thighs rippling under the Crimplene fabric of his plus-fours, and pointed a chubby finger downwards. "Behold what lays beneath us," he purred with great, greedy secretiveness.

She squinted to where he was pointing. "So? So what? It's just a big—"

"Enshut your beak, and wait. While it appears to be nothing exceptional right now, just wait until tonight.

For, according to my calculations, tonight there'll be a full moon."

"A full moon?"

"Full, bright and glowing. And, when this moon deigns to show its face, and when it sails forth across the sky above our crater, the sight you see below will shift and change, to reveal the secret that only I and Dr Schnitger have located!"

"Tonight?"

"Tonight. And, mark my words, Desdemona, when the moon reveals what it *will* reveal, then let all Glory be mine! Arrrrrrrrrrr!"

A GAP IN THE PROCEEDINGS

IN THE LATTER STRETCHES of the afternoon, Cairo Jim turned a bend in the track. He stopped, dumped his knapsack at his feet, and stared at what lay ahead.

Doris, perched on his shoulder, gave a small screech.

Jocelyn stopped also, and pushed her tangly curls away from her forehead as her eyes settled on what was before them.

At the rear, Brenda halted. Her big, watchful gaze settled on the track, and she uttered a small snort of trepidation.

The track still continued upwards, steeper than ever. It appeared to be getting even narrower, the dirt and mud trail hugging the side of Gunung Dempo so closely that it was hard to see if there *was* any track in some places.

But what was most noticeable about this new stretch of track was this: it was incredibly tangled with vines that snaked across its path and up the side of the volcano, their twisted, green tendrils spreading everywhere, over each other and into the hard, baked earth of the track, and sprouting out from the dark, volcanic rock.

"What a tangle," muttered Doris. She fluttered down from Jim's shoulder and poked her beak about in the hard, gnarled vines.

"And I thought I had problems with my curls whenever I forget my brush," said Jocelyn.

Jim crouched, the sweat running down the back of his shirt and on into his shorts. He took off his sun-spectacles and leaned – very slowly, with utmost care – over the edge of the track, and looked down.

This was the first time since they had started the trek that he had looked over the edge. The drop plummeted away, so sharply, so suddenly, that it seemed as if the sheer emptiness below had sucked away all the air around them. Down, down, down, and all the way there was nothing but air and steam. And finally, thousands of metres under all of that, he could see the distant, deathly, green blanket of the tree tops at the base of Gunung Dempo.

He moved back, closer to the vines growing on the wall of the volcano. "We'll have to step extra carefully," he said, his voice calm despite the tom-tom beating of his heart. "We can't afford to lose our footing at this altitude."

"How far do you reckon it'll be until we find the Palace?" asked Doris.

Jim stood and put his sun-spectacles back on. "Hopefully not too long."

"Before nightfall?" Jocelyn said.

"Let's put it this way," answered Jim, hitching his knapsack over his shoulder again and gazing up the track – up the thin ribbon of mud and clay almost hidden by the snarl of vines. "We really have to. It doesn't look as if there'll be any room to set up camp on the track. We need to make it to the crater before it gets dark."

"Quaaaaaaaaaoo!"

Brenda had been snorting around the vines that grew out of a flattish rock on the side of Gunung Dempo. It seemed to be smoother and more regular in shape, even though it was almost smothered by the vinery.

"Rark! What's up, Bren?"

The Wonder Camel latched her sturdy teeth onto a length of vine growing flush against the rock. She took a deep breath, clamped her nostrils tightly shut, planted her hoofs firmly on the track, and gave a huge yank with her jaws.

Away came the vine with a loud ripping noise, as its strong claspers tore from the rock.

Brenda spat the vine over the side of the volcano, and locked her teeth around another piece, just under the place where the first bit of vine had come loose. Once again, she repeated the procedure and yanked this bit of vine away.

"What's she doing?" wondered Jocelyn.

"I've no idea," said Jim, bemused. "She's more full of mysteries than any other camel I've encountered. But one thing about Brenda: she doesn't do anything without a reason."

Another strong yank, and more vine came away, only to be spat over the side of the volcano.

This happened six more times…

…and then, before everyone's eyes, the thing that

Brenda had spied under all that overgrown tangle became visible.

"Well, crack my crest and call me cuneiform," squawked Doris.

"Swoggle me sculpturally," blurted Cairo Jim.

"I'll be wing-tipped," Jocelyn gasped.

"Quaaoaaoo," snorted Brenda, spitting the last bit of vine over the side.

Together and in silence, the four of them studied what Brenda's yanking and pulling had revealed: an ornate inscription carved directly onto the side of Gunung Dempo.

"It's so detailed," said Jocelyn, her eyes wandering across the designs.

The vine-growth had not caused any severe damage to the patterns and the shapes, and most of them were easy to distinguish.

In the centre of the carved section of rock were many small and intricate patterns: deeply gouged lines that curled and bisected each other, making shapes like the footprints of a seagull in wet sand, and which ran vertically up and down the rock in seven equally spaced lines.

The rest of the flat part of the inscription was bordered by a delicate pattern of figures – tiny carvings of lizards with long, coiling tails; four dancing elephants and four dancing bulls, no bigger than a child's closed fist; small birds' heads, with spiky feathers sticking out from the tops, and other, more human types of figures:

squat little plump beings, with frowning faces and puffed-up headdresses and large round loops dangling from their ears, their hands raised to the sides of their heads and their palms turned skyward.

"Strange carvings," Jim said, gently running his hand over the border. "And warm – the rock here is very warm!"

"How old do you think it is, Jim?"

"Hard to tell, Joss. I'd have to take a sample of the stone and—"

"Rerark! *I* can tell you how old it is." Doris had been perusing the pattern of delicate shapes in the centre, and she was jerking up and down excitedly.

Jim reached down, extending his forearm, and Doris hopped up onto it. "How, my dear?"

"From the writing there. I knew at once what it was, from my studies of all ancient languages and alphabets: it's ancient Padangbujur script!"

Jocelyn gave an impressed whistle.

"Ancient epigraphy's my speciality," Doris prowked.

"What does it say?" Brenda asked telepathically.

"What does it say?" Jocelyn enquired.

"Let me enlighten you," said Doris.

Jim held his arm closer to the inscription, and she straightened herself, folded her wings behind her back, and read the seagull-like marks, loudly and learnedly.

"I am the *langgatan* built in memory of those who toiled without rest to do the bidding of the

Maharaja of Srivijaya, high atop Gunung Dempo. Their work was hard. Many of them perished to do the Maharaja's will. Long be they gone, but long shall they linger on Gunung Dempo."

"So that dates it to about 683," said Jim. "Or shortly after. Good work, Doris."

"Rark. You're very welcome."

"I wonder what sort of work it was?" Jocelyn bit her lip.

"That's why we're climbing," Jim said. "I have a feeling that if we find the answer to *that*, we'll find the answer to Schnitger's mystery." He cast an eye into the sky. Already the sun was starting to move westwards, and its rays would soon be reaching them from the other side of the volcano. "Let's continue ... we have to make the top before dark."

As they set off once again, Doris asked Jim, "What's a *langgatan*?"

He frowned, and wiped the sweat from his forehead. "I've heard the word, from archaeology school, most probably. But I can't remember. We'll look it up when we get home, OK?"

"Rark."

(Only Brenda, bringing up the rear, could remember – from her calfhood encounter with those encyclopaedias – that *langgatan* meant 'altar'. She did not impart this information at the moment, partly because the afternoon was dwindling, and partly because, as she had been tearing off those vines from the inscription, she had seen a small hole in the rock face.

Through the hole she had spied – briefly, but not briefly enough – a steamy room on the other side. In there, as the steam wafted, she was sure she had seen a low ledge that was lined neatly with human skulls.)

"Looks like the end of the track," announced Jim sadly.

"Oh no," puffed Jocelyn. She dumped her knapsack on the ground. "To come this far, only to have *this*."

"It can't be," said Doris, settling on Brenda's saddle.

Jim's shoulders sagged as he stood there, faced with the wide gap of nothingness where the track had, without any warning signs, just disappeared. "It must've been washed away by rain," he mumbled, trying not to let the disappointment choke his voice too much.

Brenda inched forward to where their part of the track finished. Cautiously she stretched her neck, and peered down into the abyss. All she could see, thousands and thousands of metres below, was distant greenery and spouts of rising, steamy mist.

"Quaaaaoooo!" she snorted angrily.

"Quaaaaoooo!"

"Quaaaaoooo!"

"Quaaaaoooo!"

"Quaaaaoooo!"

her echoing snort came back at her.

Doris flew off Brenda's saddle and across to the other side of the gap. "It's not that far," she screeched.

"About three metres. We could easily make a bridge out of branches!"

"No we couldn't," called Jim. "Look around, my dear. Where are the trees?"

It was true – there were none at all.

"It'd take us a full day to go back down to the last section of the track where there were enough sturdy trees growing. And then we'd have to cut them and haul the branches all the way back up…"

"Well," the macaw cooed, "how about the vines? There're thousands of them growing here!"

Jim pulled a bit of vine off the rock and rubbed its old, gnarled flesh between his fingers. "The problem is where do we tether it? There's only mud on this side of the track and on that side … no tree trunks sticking out, or big rocks, or anything else substantial enough to tie these onto."

"We could jump?" Jocelyn suggested in a small voice.

Jim looked at the gap, then at the enormous, eye-watering drop below. "I don't think so," he answered sadly.

Then Brenda stood and raised her beautiful head. A slight, hot breeze wafted her mane back from her neck, and her eyelashes flickered with bold defiance. She was not going to let a patch of nothingness – a gap in the proceedings – stop them!

"Allow me," she thought, the bravery rippling through her mind and out into the steaminess around them.

"Brenda?" said Jim. "What is it?"

"Rark, what's cookin', Bren?"

"*I can cover three metres,*" she telepathised. "*Fully stretched out, with my front hoofs on the track on that side, and my back hoofs on the track on this side, I can become a Wonder Camel bridge!*"

"I can't allow it," said Jim, shaking his head.

"Can't allow what?" asked Doris.

Jocelyn gave him a puzzled look.

He took off his pith helmet and fanned his face. "I ... I just had the weirdest thought – Brenda could cover that distance in front. If she put her front hoofs on that side, and her back hoofs on this side, then we could possibly... Oh, the heat must be getting to me. You can see why I nipped it in the bud!"

"Rerk, no, no, no, it's a great idea!" Doris flew back across the gap, and came to perch on the top of Brenda's head, between her ears. "What about it, Bren? Would you mind if Jim and Jocelyn Osgood climbed across you as you stretched across the gap?"

"Quaaaoooo!" She rolled her head in a wide, circular motion – sometimes the transference of ideas took such a long time!

"Oh, but we couldn't," protested Jim. "It'd be so ... so ... well, *undignified*, for a start."

Jocelyn looked at him.

"For Brenda, I mean."

"*I don't mind in the slightest,*" thought Brenda. "*We're a team, and I'm as much a part of it as everyone else.*

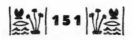 151

And if it's the only way to reach the Palace..."

"I'm sure Brenda doesn't mind in the slightest." Jocelyn rubbed Brenda's snout gently. "Do you, you lovely Bactrian?"

Brenda fluttered her eyelashes, and Jocelyn grinned.

"Besides, Jim," added Doris, "if it's the only way to reach the Palace, why shouldn't we give it a go?"

"Well..." He was still fanning his face, which had grown even hotter with the thought of what Brenda was prepared to do. "I suppose so."

"Rark, about time!"

"Quaaaaaaoooooo!"

"Good decision, Jim." Jocelyn patted his arm.

The archaeologist-poet stroked Brenda's mane. "Are you positive about this, my lovely?" He looked deeply into her wide, magnificently brown eyes.

"Quaaaaooo!"

"All right, then. First things first." He took off his knapsack. "Doris, my dear, this isn't too heavy, and it's only a short distance across the gap. Could you ferry this and Joss's over to the other side?"

Without a word, Doris took his knapsack's straps in her beak, and ascended. A few seconds later, she had gently deposited the knapsack on the track on the other side of the gap.

Without any fuss, she repeated the exercise and placed Jocelyn's knapsack beside Jim's.

"Now, Joss," said Jim, "help me take the saddlebags off Brenda's saddle. We'll throw them over to the other side before we cross, because she won't be wanting to be carrying them while she's straddling the gap."

"Good thinking," Doris said.

Jocelyn removed both saddlebags and Jim held the first one above his head. It was heavy, and it reminded Jim how good Brenda was at carrying all the weight and how she never once complained.

He squinted at the narrow track on the other side of the gap – it was only a little less than a metre wide, and his aim would have to be accurate, otherwise the saddle-bag might easily topple over the side.

"One, two, THREE!" he shouted. Up went the bag, over the gap it sailed, down onto the track it skidded.

They all watched as the bag rolled over and over, along the centre of the track. Eventually it came to a stop, muddied but otherwise unharmed.

"One down, one to go." Jim lifted the other saddle-bag and, with a deep breath and taking measured aim, he hoisted this one also.

But this time one of the straps on the bag caught his wrist as he let go, and the bag was sent off course. Over the gap it went, smashing down onto the other side, and sliding at an angle along the track.

Everyone watched as the bag kept sliding ... on and on and on...

...and over the edge!

Down, down, down, forever down, falling like a dead thing shot out of the skies. It turned over and over, its straps flapping wildly, as it travelled silently through the abyss of misty airspace.

Then, as all eyes watched it growing smaller and smaller, it disappeared into one of the thick columns of rising steam.

"Call me butterfingers," said Jim. "I'm sorry, everyone, we can't afford to lose any supplies, and there goes nearly half of what we had."

Doris soared over to the other side of the track, and poked her beak into the remaining saddlebag. "Don't worry, Jim! The food's all in here! The other bag just had the tents and some of your archaeological equipment in it!"

Jocelyn rubbed his arm reassuringly. "Not to worry," she soothed. "We've got the most important things, haven't we? We can always find some sheltered spot to sleep in, once we arrive at the ruins."

Jim looked at his friend, and her thoughtfulness made him feel less annoyed with himself.

"Rerk!" cried Doris. "Cut that out, you two!"

Brenda moved to the edge of the track, to the point where the gap commenced. *Now,* she thought, her heart beating fiercely and her humps tingling with more apprehension than she had felt in a long, long time, *now is the time to do it.*

"Are you ready, my lovely?" Jim asked.

"As ready as I'll ever be," she thought, trembling as she raised herself so that, in rare Wonder Camel fashion, she was standing straight up on her two back legs.

She took a step towards the edge, and raised her front hoofs straight up above her head. Then she balanced, for the briefest and most hoof-sweating of moments, and took a deep, brave breath.

It's all in the way of falling, she thought, as she let herself topple forward towards the gap.

RESCUED BY RAPACIOUSNESS

DESDEMONA WAS PERCHED ON THE TOP of a crumbled wall, her slitted eyes glued to the Twoctet building their huts, when she heard the noise.

"Craaaaaark! What was that?"

Bone opened one eye (he had been in a half-slumber, dreaming of wealth and fame and massive global domination and lamingtons) and scowled at her. "What was what?"

"That noise. I just heard it. Sounded like a big thud, somewhere over them walls, outside the grounds here."

The fleshy megalomaniac rolled over and pulled his fez down over his eyes. "Probably just a tree falling, you uncouth utensil of unctuosity. Trees are always falling in the sinister jungles."

"Nope, that was no tree falling. Not unless trees make snorting sounds." Her eyes throbbed with curiosity.

"Well, if it bothers you so much, fly off and find out. Put your cotton wool to rest."

"I think I will," she croaked. "I think I'll do just that…"

"*Quuuuaaaaaaaaaooooooo!*"

"Brenda! My lovely, are you safe?"

"Raaark, hang on tight, Bren!"

The Wonder Camel had fallen across the gap, huge and silent, like a tree in the jungle might have fallen after two hundred years of growth. Her front hoofs had smacked hard down onto the very edge of the track on the other side of the gap, and her back feet had risen to the occasion, using their double-jointedness to arch way back and give her hoofs on the opposite edge a strong, firm hold.

But her situation was not secure.

"Quaaaooooo!" she snorted again, as she felt her front left hoof sliding back towards her – towards the gap!

Jim's eyes widened, and he ripped off his sun-spectacles. "Take a deep breath," he called. "And imagine this, my lovely: imagine that you're as light as a small balloon, that there's no weight in your humps or your belly, and you're filled with air."

Brenda closed her long lashes and concentrated hard on the image Jim had suggested. She sensed nothing in her mind, except for the weightlessness of her body.

Her hoof slid a little more, and she heard the dry, cakey mud crumbling from under it, and falling down, far away into the abyss!

"Concentrate, my lovely!" She heard Jim's urging voice, full of support and desperate kindness and caring, and still she tried to imagine herself without any mass, and willed herself to put that hoof back firmly onto the track.

Doris fluttered close by her haunches. "You can do it, Bren!"

"Don't be distracted," Jocelyn called.

And then, as though it were the easiest thing in the world, she felt her hoof sliding back into place on the edge of the track.

She pushed it firmly into the half-dried mud, pushed it as much as she could until she felt it was as entrenched as her other front hoof. Only when she was absolutely certain that she was well and truly settled, balanced and confident, did she open her eyes.

Cairo Jim knelt by her back hoofs. "Are you all right, Brenda? Roll your head if you feel you are."

Her beautiful big head rolled once around. Then she settled the very tip of her chin on the edge of the track, in between her front legs.

"Time to cross, Jim," said Jocelyn. "Before she tires and loses concentration."

"Right," he said quietly, his vocal chords sounding like they were lined with sandpaper. "Let's cross our Wonder Camel bridge." He looked up at Jocelyn, and saw the creases of trepidation in her forehead. "Like to go first, Joss?"

She looked down into his clouded, blue eyes, and for a moment the trepidation vanished. "No," she answered, giving him a half-smile. "After you, my friend. I'll pick up a few pointers from your journey."

"Rightio."

"Quuuaaaaoooooo!" came a snort of please-hurry-I've-never-been-in-this-position-before!

He pocketed his sun-spectacles (in case they fell off while he was crossing Brenda) and slowly leaned forward, extending his arms until they were lying flat against Brenda's rear legs. She pressed her tail close to her flanks so that it wouldn't get in the way.

"Here goes," grunted Jim. He moved his arms forward, gripping Brenda's upper rear legs, and at the same time he crawled slowly forwards.

Now his knees were touching her hoofs. He raised first his right knee and settled it as gently as he could onto Brenda's rear right hoof and her double-jointed foot. Then he did the same with his left knee, onto her left foot.

Brenda stiffened slightly, but then, in the next instant, she forced herself to return to her state of calm weightlessness.

"So far so..." Jim stopped muttering, and edged his knees forward, bit by bit, moment by moment, until his whole body weight was off the track and resting on the backs of Brenda's legs.

The only thing that separated him from the void below, from the drop of many thousands of life-sucking metres, from a dreadful and agonising plummeting that he had never dared contemplate in his life, was his friend the Wonder Camel.

"*Come on, Jim,*" Brenda urged with her powerful mind. "*Up onto my rear hump, now.*"

The archaeologist-poet moved his hands up and grabbed onto the hem of her macramé saddle. Using his biceps, he pulled himself into a position where he was kneeling against her upper legs.

And, in a quick movement of well-judged balancing, he half-sprang, half-hoisted himself up onto the back of her saddle.

"Rark! Way to go, Jim!"

Jocelyn watched, her breath hardly exiting her fine nostrils.

The top of Jim's body – his chest and torso and arms – was lying across the back of Brenda's saddle, on top of her rear hump. He paused and felt a bead of sweat trickle down his forehead.

Now all he had to do was reach forward and slowly pull himself across her fore hump, over her neck and onto the opposite side of the track.

This he started to do, moving with butterfly-softness, as he came closer and closer to the front of Brenda.

Then he came unstuck!

It all happened so quickly: one second he was atop Brenda's front hump; the next, he overbalanced to the right and was toppling helplessly down her side.

"Oooooooooooeeeer!" he cried.

"Jim!" Jocelyn screamed.

"Ooooooooeeeeeeer!" Down he slid, his fingers trying to clutch at the macramé saddle covering. But there was nothing to hook his fingers around – the side of the saddle was one smooth, tightly knotted surface.

Then he fell, completely away from Brenda's body, down into the abyss.

"Scraaaaaaaaaaaaaaark!" Doris's heart was about to burst through her feathers.

Instants of time flashed: he looked up, saw the underside of Brenda's belly and her saddle straps around it, felt the gusts of hot air rising from the endless void beneath him, smelled the rotting, steamy vegetation and the moist volcanoside, watched as his pith helmet blew off and away into the air, and—

—miraculously, at the last possible moment before he would lose his chance, his hand shot upwards, slipping into the space in Brenda's stirrup. His fingers curled tightly around the brass, and there he dangled, his legs kicking against the air.

"Quaaaaoooooo!" Brenda bowed a bit in the middle by the jolting arrival of Jim's mass. She shut her eyes and concentrated on being light.

Doris flapped around, feeling helpless at the plight of her best human friend. She knew that all she could do would be to try and bump him upwards again, by flying under him and up against him, over and over. But she knew this would be more of a hindrance than a help. She needed to be bigger at this point in time. "Rark, Jocelyn Osgood, Jocelyn Osgood, do something!"

"Don't fret, Doris." Jocelyn was already on her knees, and kneeling on Brenda's rear legs.

"Be careful, Joss," moaned Jim, his fingers moist and slippery.

Brenda could feel Jim squirming. She did her best to stay calm and still.

Jocelyn edged forward. Reaching out, she gripped Brenda's flanks and hauled herself slowly up until her chin was resting on the top of Brenda's rear hump.

"Hang in there, Jim!" screeched Doris.

"I'm hanging," he grunted, his legs flailing all around him.

Jocelyn arched herself up and over, onto the ridge that ran along the top of Brenda's saddle, in between her humps. She settled her weight onto Brenda as if she were no heavier than a feather. "Are you managing, Brenda?" she whispered, pushing a renegade tangly lock of hair out of her eyes.

"Quaaaoooo," snorted the Wonder Camel, but with a hint of worry in her throat.

"Now, Jim," Jocelyn called in her cool, confident Flight Attendant's voice, "listen carefully: how securely is Brenda's saddle fastened around her?"

"V ... v ... very securely. I strapped it round myself." His voice was breathy and gasping for air.

"Good. I'm going to extend my arm down to you. Wait till my hand is right next to yours – wait till I'm touching your knuckles – then swiftly let go of the stirrup and grab hold of my hand! I'll pull you back up. Got it?"

"Please hurry, Joss!"

Doris landed on the track close to Brenda's snout, and wafted air over her friend's face with her wings. "You coping, Bren?"

Brenda looked at her. Then she closed her eyes,

and Doris saw the enormous beads of sweat dotting her eyelashes.

"Rark, quickly! Brenda's feeling the strain!"

"Ready, Jim?"

"Ugh ... ready."

Her right hand was trembling as she lowered it slowly down past Brenda's side. Her other hand gripped the top of the saddle so tightly, her knuckles were turning white.

Down went the hand of Jocelyn Osgood.

Jim looked up, watching her long fingers approaching, moving through the void as if in slow motion.

"Nearly there," she thought. She pushed down a few more millimetres.

But, just as her hand was about to brush Jim's knuckles, a sharp pain shot into her other hand. "Ow! My thumb!"

Her splinted, injured thumb felt as if a knife had been plunged into it.

The sudden ferocity of the stabbing pain threw her. She pulled her right hand back towards her, sat upright, and lost her balance.

And fell over the side!

On the crumbled wall only five metres above, Desdemona had watched all of this with a growing, malevolent delight. Her eyes throbbed merrily at the sight of the 'goody-goodies' (as she had referred to them countless times in conversations with Bone) finding themselves in such straits.

 163

When she saw Jocelyn Osgood fall off the Wonder Camel, she raised her wings and flew back to tell the good news to her adipose companion.

"Jim! Don't move your leg!"

Cairo Jim looked down. There, gripping onto the very tip of one of his Sahara boots, dangled Jocelyn.

"*Quaaaaaaoooooooo!*" Brenda was not sure how much longer she could bear their combined weight suspended over the nothingness below.

Doris watched, helpless, squawkless, screechless...

"How did you get there?" Jim called, as her weight stretched his body tauter and tauter.

"You were thrashing about. Your feet. Caught you on the way down. I'm losing grip, Jim."

"No!"

"Can't use this hand ... the thumb's weakened it ... can only hold on with this one ..."

Jim closed his eyes. A torrent of perspiration filled his shirt, and his mind reeled, trying to work out what to do next.

"*Hurry,*" Brenda thought urgently. "*Please, try and come back up ... my hoofs are sliding inwards!*"

Jim felt Brenda's body move. He looked up and saw her front hoofs creeping deeper into the mud, closer to the lip of the gap.

"*Jim!*" Jocelyn's cry was almost hoarse in its franticness. His eyes shot down to see two of her fingers peeling off the tip of his boot, one by one.

"No, Joss! Hang on! Try with all your—"

"Don't give up, Jocelyn Osgood!" Doris took off from the track and started flying all around her.

Jim felt the brass of the stirrup digging hard into his hand. He winced in pain.

A hot breeze blew the damp curls off Jocelyn's face. "Can't hold … any longer!" Another finger slid off his boot, leaving her clinging by only her index finger and thumb.

Jocelyn looked up, and her eyes met Jim's. Briefly, for a moment he would never forget, he saw right into her clear irises, past the fear and the terror and the desperate panic.

"Remember me, Jim," she whispered.

"*JOSS, NO!*"

"I'd never have missed this for the—"

There was no more; in the silence, the strength in her fingers left her. She was gone.

Jim, Doris and Brenda watched, their heartbeats almost deafening them, as Jocelyn grew smaller and smaller while she fell farther and farther. The pale blue of her jodhpurs was the last thing they could see. It finally disappeared into a clump of green denseness growing out from the side of the volcano, hundreds of metres below.

All throughout her fall, she had made no sound whatsoever.

"Crark! Losers!"

"This'd better be good, you dimwitted deposit of

dumbness, to get me off my comfy patch of leaves."

Desdemona perched on the wall. "Look down there, grumble-cheeks."

Bone pushed his fat neck over the side of the wall, and saw Jim dangling from Brenda, with Doris circling frantically around.

"Well, well, well," he purred, his eyes lighting up at the sight of his arch nemesis. "It seems we have visitors. Arrrrr."

Jim's shoulders were heaving as he hung there, weak and hopeless.

"Oh, looky, Desdemona. It seems that Mr Archaeology is sobbing. How wretched for the man."

"Let's get some boulders, my Captain. We can get the Twoctet to hurl some big boulders over the side. Finish the three of 'em off, bad and proper."

Bone puffed on his cigar, and a creeping smile spread across his lips. "No, Desdemona. Let's get the Twoctet to get some of those long bamboo poles they've been chopping, and run down the track to slide them under the camel. I think we should *rescue* Jim and his little entourage."

"Crark! Rescue 'em? We've been battlin' against 'em for years. They always stop you in your plans! Are you addled?"

"Oh, no, no, no. I want to *rescue* them so that they can witness, by tonight's moonfall, the greatness I have rediscovered. Only then, when Cairo Jim has seen that I have won, will his miserable little life – and the lives of that camel and that gaudy macaw – come to a complete and pathetic end."

"Heh heh heh," sniggered the raven. "That'll be worth watchin'! I'll get the Twoctet right away, with them poles!" Off she flew to the women below.

"Finally," whispered Neptune Bone, as he watched his helpless adversaries, "the world turns to the beating of *my* drums! What a symphony of sweetness it shall be! *Aaaaaaaarrrrrrrrrrr!*"

THE PALACE OF SRIVIJAYA

"JIM! JIM! Are these ... the Amazons?"⋆

Cairo Jim, walking next to Brenda and surrounded by the Twoctet, who were leading them up the last section of the track, shook his head. "I don't think so, Doris. I don't think the Amazons ever wore tracksuits."

Brenda trudged on sadly next to Jim. Like Jim and Doris, she kept thinking of Jocelyn and what had befallen her.

As they all neared a rise in the track, Fatimé Breeches turned to them. She lowered her bamboo pole and pointed with it to the crumbled wall half hidden by the overgrown vines and weeds. "Here," she said throatily, "is where we take you to Mr Glamourdust."

"Mr Glamourdust," repeated the other women rapturously.

"Mr Glamourdust?" squawked Doris in Jim's ear.

He shook his head, and the women led them beyond the crumbled wall and into the Palace grounds.

"Arrrr, well look what the gals dragged in!"

"Crark! The losers have come hither!"

⋆ The legendary ancient race of warrior women.

"Thank you, ladies," Bone purred. "Now go and stand guard at equal distances around the walls – these dangerous captives must *not* escape!"

"Yes, Mr Glamourdust," came Fatimé's throaty reply. She marched the other women away and organised them as per his orders.

Jim ripped off his sun-spectacles, which he had put on again after his rescue. "Bone! What in the name of Schliemann are you doing here?"

Doris became agitated atop Jim's shoulder. "You great, deceitful windbag! We thought you were in prison!"

Desdemona shot across and landed on Jim's head, digging her talons in more than was necessary. "Enshut your beak, Dolly-bird," she croaked, her eyes throbbing cruelly as she swatted at Doris with her greasy wing. "You're in no position to squawk!"

"Call her off, Bone!" shouted Jim.

Bone raised a heavy eyebrow and smirked. Then he snapped his chubby fingers moistly. "Come, Desdemona, away from all that misguided *goodness*." He pronounced the word as though it was something smelly he had stepped in and now it was stuck to the sole of his shoe.

She dug her talons in extra hard – Jim winced sharply – and flew back to land on Bone's fez.

The obese man waved his hand across the grounds. "Here I am known as Mr Glamourdust," he told them. "Welcome, you dregs of all things bright and beautiful, to the wondrous grounds of the Palace of the Maharaja of Srivijaya!"

Jim, Doris and Brenda diverted their attention from Bone and the raven, and let their eyes wander around the Palace grounds.

Most of the place was in ruins. They were standing in some sort of enormous overgrown courtyard, which might once have been a grand terrace. Big weeds sprouted through the cracked, orange-coloured tiles on the ground, and vines riddled the short walls enclosing this area.

Over to one side, a towering camphorwood tree had broken through another, taller wall and was growing out through the broken stones.

Behind all of this rose the remains of a half-fallen tower. Here and there some windows, with pointed tops and rounded sides, had become the homes to lush, drooping ferns.

Brenda snorted quietly. "Look! Look at that small patch of wall there, by the ruined doorway! See the tiles around it?"

"Look, Doris, Brenda," said Jim. "Look at those beautiful little tiles by the ruined doorway."

All around the door frame were dozens of white and blue and yellow diamond-shaped tiles – an intricate mosaic that followed the shape of the door.

"Arrr," said Bone. "I'd bet my fez that in its glory-days, the whole Palace would've been covered with such decoration."

From the gaps and cracks in the tiled floor, dotted around the courtyard, small shafts of steam rose up, wafting into the moist air.

Along the walls sat more than twenty big pots. The ones that hadn't cracked and fallen apart were tall and voluminous, and sprouted wild orchids from their rims.

Doris noticed something. "Rark, see on that ledge up there! Those flowers!"

Jim and Brenda looked up to the ledge that had been made when another big section of wall hand, once upon a time, collapsed. "The *Rafflesia gargantua indestructibilia*. There must be a dozen, and they're the hugest we've seen!"

These specimens were even more enormous than the others – the width of their lobe-petalled orange, yellow and purply-red-flecked flowers was about two and a half metres, and their cups were almost two metres deep.

"Stinky things," sneered Bone, blowing cigar smoke contemptuously into the air.

Jim turned to him. "Bone, please, you and those women have to help us. We have to find our friend. She ... she fell, and..." His voice choked on him, and no more words came.

Bone sneered even more. "Your *friend*? You mean you still waste your time on such outdated concepts such as friendship? Ha!"

"It was Jocelyn Osgood, that's who it was," gloated Desdemona.

Suddenly Bone's beard bristled. "Jocelyn Osgood? JOCELYN OSGOOD? Is that right, Cairo Jim?"

He nodded.

"She fell," said Doris. "Into the jungle down there somewhere. We have to look for her."

Bone's beard continued to bristle as he remembered how, long ago, so long ago that it seemed like another lifetime, he and Jim and Jocelyn Osgood had been the best of friends. Way back in the days when Bone and Jim were at Archaeology School, and Jocelyn was training to be a Flight Attendant with Valkyrian Airways.

The three of them had been close, had enjoyed many outings and activities together, until that dreadful day when it had become clear to the young Bone that Jocelyn Osgood obviously preferred the company of Cairo Jim to his. He had felt crushed, humiliated, itchy (because of some new underpants his mother had bought for him), and he had stormed off in a mighty huff.

That was the day he had decided to turn his back on such things as friendship and goodness and personal cleanliness, and to pursue his number-one interest: the lust for massive wealth and widespread glorification.

Jim's voice snapped him back from his memories: "Yes … she lost her plane and now… I don't know, she may even still be alive down there…"

"You infernal optimist!" Bone growled at him. He wiped the sweat from his forehead, and his beard started to return to an unbristly state. "She's probably broken into a thousand little pieces. Smashed to smithereens by the sinister forest! Arrrrr."

Brenda shuddered.

"Please," urged Jim. "Let's take the women down there and look for her. I owe her at least that much."

"We'll do no such thing. We are here, not for you and your goody-goody buddies, but for my ends and means. Tonight you shall witness my greatest discovery!"

"What on earth are you hoping to find?" Jim almost spat the question at him. "This place is in ruins!"

Bone smiled, and Desdemona listened for an answer. She, too, was almost delirious with curiosity. "There's one place here you haven't seen yet," he hissed. "Come, and look, and learn a tad more about my plans."

With a pompous swagger he led them to the edge of the courtyard. He leaned on the ledge that bordered the area, and looked over. "See? Down there is something that will interest you."

Jim, Doris and Brenda looked over the ledge as well. Desdemona cast a blood-red eye at the scene below.

There, stretching out to fill this part of the volcano's crater from wall to wall, was a huge expanse of bright blue, sparkling water!

The fading sunlight of the afternoon cast glinting beams onto the surface, forming tiny, bright, pin-pricks of light on the ripples that appeared and then disappeared.

"A ... a lake!" exclaimed Jim.

"A lagoon," Bone corrected him in a superior tone. "A human-made lagoon. Ordered to be built down there by the Maharaja of Srivijaya himself!"

"Is this what you were after?" asked Jim. "A *lagoon*?"

Bone turned to him, and blew a column of smoke directly into his face. "Like me, this lagoon does not reveal all of itself. At least, not yet. No, my hated associate, tonight, when the moon is full, you and your pathetic little party shall witness much more to this lagoon than meets the eye. And you shall witness another page in my ongoing book of Greatness!"

"But what? How?"

"Enough, Cairo Jim! Desdemona?"

"Yep?"

"Get the Twoctet to escort our captives to their temporary accommodation. I want them to have a first-class position to behold the greatness that the lagoon will reveal when the full moon rises tonight. After all, it will be the very last thing they shall behold on this earth!"

And, in a wash of terror, the colour drained from the faces of Jim, Doris and Brenda.

MOONLIGHT BECOMES ERGGGH!

DORIS STRUGGLED AGAINST the raven's strong wings. "No! Let go of me, you fleabag! You can't put me in there!"

"Shut up and get in!"

Desdemona was forcing Doris into the cup of one of the *Rafflesia gargantua indestructibilia*. On each side of her, Jim and Brenda were also being forced into their own flower-cups by Kaynarca and Dënise. Man, macaw and Wonder Camel had all been bound tightly with pieces of hard, coarse jungle vine and, in such circumstances, struggling was merely a waste of time and energy.

"You won't get away with this," Doris screeched. "I don't know how, but when I get out of here, I'll see you caught and incarcerated!"

"And I'm Desi Arnaz," croaked the raven. She pushed Doris down.

The huge, lobe-like petals *flooomped* upwards, coming together around Doris's neckfeathers. It was a snug fit – not strangulating – and only the macaw's head was sticking out above the tops of the petals.

"Bye bye, flower flier," rasped Desdemona. "You'll have a great view of the show tonight, when the moon's full!" She raised her wings and flew off to join her master.

"Illiterate," muttered Doris. She swivelled her neck as much as she could. To the right she saw Jim's head, also sticking up from the inside of one of the *Rafflesia* cups. The lobe-petals had similarly imprisoned him from the neck downwards.

"Quaaaooo." To the left, Brenda was incarcerated as well – her snout and head were the only parts of her visible from within the flower. She had been placed inside the widest, fattest, sturdiest of the *Rafflesia gargantua indestructibilia* plants, and she was as helpless as her two friends. The might of the Twoctet had been too much even for her.

Cairo Jim tried to struggle against the vines that held him, but it was no use: the harder he squirmed, the tighter the lobe-petals clamped about his neck. Their hardness was unrelenting, and he decided not to continue struggling in case his oxygen supply was cut off by the lethal plants.

Just then, Doris remembered something. "Hey, Jim, Bren! What was it that we found out about these flowers earlier? About how they trap their prey?"

Brenda closed her eyes, and dredged up the information from her memory, sending it out so that Jim could grasp it.

"Inside the cups of *Rafflesia gargantua indestructibilia* there are contained sacs of a lethal acid which kills any parasites or predators that get trapped within. This acid, known as 'indestructibilia juice', is only secreted whenever the moon is full. Prey is trapped within the cup of the flower until such times, when the indestructibilia juice is released. If the prey has not died of suffocation already, the indestructibilia juice will drown it and break it down so that the *Rafflesia gargantua indestructibilia* can digest it."

"I guess that's when the dreadful smell comes," said Doris, "when the indestructibilia juice is let off. Oh, well, at least we don't have to worry about— REEEAAAAARRRRKKKKKKKKKK!"

"You're thinking what I'm thinking," thought Brenda.

"Tonight's the full moon," gasped Jim. "Tonight we see the secret of the lagoon, by the light of the full moon!"

"And we become dinner," Doris said gravely, as the sun began to set over the rim of the crater walls.

Fatimé Breeches stood with her broad back firmly against the crumbled, vine-infested wall, watching.

Her stern eye kept close check on her seven Team mates as they, too, stood guard over the Palace courtyard. From time to time she glanced up, checking that the three captives were still securely incarcerated within the lobe-petals of the gigantic flowers up on the ledge. Sometimes she gazed down at the ever-so-gently-lapping lagoon at the bottom of the crater.

The sun had disappeared now, having slid below the rim of the crater. Soon it would slide even further, and vanish over the horizon.

Up in the evening sky the moon began to emerge,

slowly and regally, like a great ship about to embark across an ocean of stars.

Down below, deep inside Fatimé Breeches, a curious, niggling sensation began to emerge, just as gradually as the moon began its journey across the sky...

The leaves rustled. Small twigs gave way under the movement and snapped softly. Somewhere far away a flock of Malay parrots shrieked frantically into the fast-approaching darkness.

Jocelyn Osgood opened her eyes and rolled onto her side. She was in a gloomy place – a place of soft under-growth and bracken, of cushioning leaves and lush ferns.

With a groan, she sat upright and rubbed her head. Her thumb still ached, dully but persistently, and there was another ache in her left leg. She hitched up the lower part of her torn jodhpurs and saw that she had many small scratches. That must have happened a while ago, she thought, inspecting the dried blood smears on her jodhpurs.

Her arm was scratched, too, and her shirtsleeve had been torn from shoulder to elbow. She was bruised all along the length of her left side, and – not that she could see it – her cheekbone on this side of her face was a deep purple colour.

Her head was pounding, and she didn't know where she was. The last thing she could remember – and it took great effort to remember even this – was space: endless, hot, steamy space.

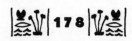

Painfully she turned her head to the right. Darkness. Some sort of dim wall with vines hanging down it. As her eyes adjusted to the gloom, she saw on this wall little rivulets of sparkling water seeping down the rock face. She extended her good hand and felt one of these. Wet, and warm, but not hot. Raising her fingertips to her scratched lips, she tasted the water. It was good.

She slowly raised herself to a kneeling position, and cupped her hands under one of the springs. Her throat was dry, but she managed to gulp down enough water to take away the parched, burning feeling in her mouth.

She sat back and turned her head the other way. There was no wall on that side, only a great dark void that stretched away. In the last remaining, weak glimmers of sunlight, she could just make out the tops of the trees, far off and below.

She knew where she was, now: somehow she had landed in a small outcrop of tree and bush that must have been protruding from the side of the volcano.

She had survived.

She closed her eyes. For a moment she was overjoyed that she was still alive, but almost at once this gave way to a feeling of hopeless desolation. She was alive for now, but how long would that last?

She was stuck, here in a place where the chance of rescue would be more than remote.

And then she heard it.

A sound. A noise.

Was it footsteps?

Her eyes shot open, and she concentrated fiercely. The sound had stopped. All she could hear was the drip-drip-dripping of the water from the side of the volcano.

Then, all around her, like a cloud-crowd moving in, came the misty light. The peculiar shapes of the vapours came to visit Jocelyn Osgood.

She couldn't tell from which direction the light first came. When she looked, she saw it moving up from the valley below in a long cluster, stretching and gliding, hesitantly sometimes and directly at other times. But it was also descending from the upper reaches of Gunung Dempo: a line of barely distinguishable shapes.

As she blinked and looked again, she thought she could see the shadowy but bright outlines of human forms in its midst.

Silently it came, this procession of light and vague figures. Floating and wafting, coming closer and closer, all around closer, to Jocelyn in her shelter.

She was breathing quickly now ... there was no doubt in her mind that this was a visitation to her.

All about her, the evening gloom had gone, washed away by the arrival of this misty lighted force.

And then the procession halted. The light hung about her, swamping everything in its glow.

Jocelyn could feel her heart beating heavily against her ribs. Her leafy shelter was filled with the light and the mist, and a great, expectant silence.

Gradually, through all of this, one shape gently emerged between Jocelyn and the cliff. Wisps of mist evaporated, and strands of light joined together to form the shape – the outline only – of a man.

Jocelyn gasped, and tried to move away, but some-how – without making any physical contact with her – the figure stopped her.

And, even though she couldn't see any mouth or other obvious features in the region that she knew was the man's head, she heard him speak to her, not in a voice, but in the chimings of many faint bells:

"Be not afraid, be not scared. We are the spirits of Gunung Dempo. We have watched you and we are with you now."

Jocelyn took a deep breath.

"We saw your flying wings when you crashed. We saw you sleeping in your little, soft house."

"You are spirits?" Jocelyn said, her spine suddenly cold.

"Do you remember the *langgatan* you and your friends found on your journey?"

"I do."

"That is our *langgatan*. We are the spirits of the workers who toiled for the Maharaja. We are the ones who have never left the mountain."

All at once, Jocelyn was immensely sad for her glowing, shadowy visitors. Her spine started feeling less cold. "Long be you gone, but long shall you linger on Gunung Dempo," she said, remembering the inscription on the *langgatan*.

"Our spirits remain here, to keep company with

the spirit of the volcano. We were crushed by one man. The volcano was crushed by time."

"Which is why it's extinct?"

The figure wafted slightly, like a candle flame in a small breeze. "We are here to help you," came its chime again. "We will reunite you with your friends."

Now Jocelyn's spine was positively tingling, as if a dozen volts of electricity had been zapped through it.

"Thank you, thank you!"

"Come with us," the chime continued. The outline of the figure changed for a few seconds, and Jocelyn realised that it had been sitting by her, and now it was standing between her and the rock face. "We know Gunung Dempo inside and outside. Let us take you with us, through the inside."

Her eyes widened, and then widened even further, when she saw what happened next. Maybe she was suffering from shock after the fall, she thought. Maybe she was seeing things.

There in front of her, with a quiet, gravelly crunching, a whole section of the rock face slid inwards, into the centre of the mountain.

Beyond, through the trailing vines (which, now that this bit of the rock face had moved, were just like a dangling curtain), Jocelyn could see a corridor, hewn into the interior of Gunung Dempo and illuminated by thousands of misty shapes like the one with which she had been in communication.

A sea of soft chiming swelled out from inside the mountain.

"Come," beckoned the figure nearest her, with a reassuring glow. "The Maharaja did not destroy our spirits, only our bodies, and our spirits are eternally searching for what is just. Let us reunite you with what you need the most."

As she rose to follow him into the volcano, a sense of calmness flooded through Jocelyn Osgood's body. Inside the volcano it was warm and steamy. Slowly, with the same gravelly crunching, the rock-face door closed behind her.

TIDE ON MY SIDE

LIKE A COLOSSAL MISSIVE FROM the heavens, the full moon sailed majestically across the upper realms of the skies.

Neptune Bone watched it impatiently as it soared slowly overhead. According to what he had copied into his black pocket-journal from Dr Schnitger's diaries, all would be revealed the moment the moon was directly above the very centre of the crater.

Desdemona flitted onto a decaying window sill by his elbow. "Hey, big boy," she croaked.

"What, you interrupting item of idiocy?"

"Those Twoctets are gettin' restless. They're moanin' for more of your tea. All except for that Breeches woman. She's just standin' there against the wall with this weird look in her peepers. She looks uglier than normal."

Bone reached into the pocket in his plus-fours trousers. "Here," he said, distractedly handing her the tube containing the Obsequious Pills. "Give them their tea. Three cups each, this time. But only pop two of these pills into the samovar when you brew it."

The raven took the tube. "Two, eh?"

"Hurry, do it now! I don't want you and your distractions to come between me and that other, lesser brilliant body up there."

"The only thing you and the moon have in common is your size," she muttered before flying off to the samovar and the thirsty Turkish women.

Up on their ledge, encased in the bulbs of the *Rafflesia gargantua indestructibilia*, Jim, Doris and Brenda waited and watched.

"The moon's rising, all right," Jim said. "How are you both doing?"

Doris squirmed and wriggled her claws around inside the flower. "All right so far," she fretted. "Can't feel any of that indestructibilia juice seeping out yet."

"Brenda, my lovely?"

"Quaaaoooo," she snorted, agreeing with Doris but anxious nonetheless.

Jim stretched his neck and called out. "Bone! Hey! What's going on? What are we waiting for?"

Bone turned to them, up on their ledge. He bent down and lifted an old movie director's megaphone (which he had taken out of his Travelling Trunkette), placing it importantly to his lips. "It is time, I suppose, to divulge much of my knowledge to you non-entities. I am a generous man, after all, and I have always believed that lives should not be ended in total ignorance."

"Oooh," Doris bristled, "if I wasn't shut away in this thing, he'd be getting a mouthful of feathered fury!"

"Let me set the scene a tad more fully for you," boomed the fleshy man through the megaphone. "As you can see, the moon is indeed rising. According to Dr Schnitger, once a month, on a night such as this – when the moon is at its fullest and roundest and most bright and shining – the miracle of the Maharaja of Srivijaya's grandeur is revealed."

"What grandeur?" shouted Jim. "What's so grand about a lagoon?"

Desdemona flew back to join Bone. "Yeah, go on, tell us."

"Oh," he declaimed, his voice vibrating loudly (and making Desdemona's eyes throb all the harder), "I'll do better than that. Watch!"

He pointed a pudgy finger up to the sky, as the moon moved directly across a point that was above the exact centre of the grounds of the Palace – the very middle of the crater.

Jim, Doris and Brenda watched it, and felt the temperature inside the bulb of their *Rafflesia gargantua indestructibilia* grow fractionally hotter.

"It's arrived," Bone announced, swinging his pointing finger down to the lagoon. "And here is what I have come for!"

Spreading through time, the strong, direct beams from the moon shone down onto the still lagoon. The surface of the water glowed, and its colour changed, gently, silently, from blue to white.

"Swoggle me shiningly," whispered Cairo Jim.

"Now here it comes," Bone hissed, his eyes wide and full of greedy anticipation.

"Jim!" came a faint voice from behind Jim's flower-prison.

He swivelled his head as far as he could. There, surrounded by an iridescent glow of strangely shaped light, stood Jocelyn.

Jim's mouth fell open. Doris and Brenda saw him, and turned their heads to see what he had been looking at. When they saw Jocelyn there, behind the clusters of *Rafflesia*, they were struck squawkless and snortless.

"J-J-Joss!" Jim managed to stammer, his heart overjoyed at the sight of her. "How did you—?"

"I don't really know," she whispered. "I had help, but I'm not sure." She rubbed her head. "Somehow it all seems like a dream ..."

The light and the mist bathed her in its glow, and she heard a voice, a voice like chiming bells, close by her ear: "Be with those you need. There will be a way. There will always be a way."

So it was that the mist and the light evaporated, melting back into the hole in the side of the volcano through which it had brought Jocelyn.

"Jim! Down there! Is that ... *Neptune Bone*?"

"Unfortunately. Look! Look at the lagoon!"

"Arrrrr," murmured Bone, his eyes transfixed by the sight of the water below him. The colour of the surface continued to change, slowly, silently, gradually and, with it, Bone's eyes changed also, growing wilder and wilder.

"Here it comes!" he whispered breathlessly.

Now the lagoon was going from white to another colour – a bright, almost dazzling yellow.

"That light," Jocelyn said, shielding her eyes. "It's the same light I saw when I crashed the plane!"

"And the same sort of brightness we saw from down on the track, when those beams were shooting up from inside the crater!" added Jim.

"Quaaaooo," Brenda snorted, as the inside of her bulb grew hotter and hotter…

"Showtime!" cried Bone.

The lagoon was now brilliant and yellow, and something else was happening: great clusters of bubbles were rising to the surface, exploding into the air with loud, hollow POPPING sounds.

Everywhere across the lagoon, the bubbles rose and exploded. Soon the body of water looked like an enormous saucepan full of boiling soup.

"Just as Dr Schnitger described," Bone boomed through the megaphone. "Now, watch this!"

As quickly as the bubbles had come, they subsided again. And the water in the lagoon began to drain, speedily, with a sucking, gurgling sound so loud it bore fiercely into everyone's ear holes.

SQQQUUUUEEEEELLLLLLCCCCCHHHHHHHH!

"Arrrr," moaned Bone, as the water disappeared, down, down, gurglingly down into the bottom of the lagoon and beyond, deep under the floor of the crater of Gunung Dempo.

"MY DESTINY!" Bone shouted. He fell to his knees and beheld the emptied, damp floor of the lagoon.

Cairo Jim gasped so loudly he thought he would burst through the *Rafflesia*.

Doris screeched raucously in amazement.

Brenda sucked the air into her nostrils, hardly able to comprehend what she could see down there.

Jocelyn stood still, dazed and flabbergasted.

Desdemona couldn't move a feather, and even the fleas within her plumage could not bite or annoy her, so overcome with awe were they.

All the women of the Turkish Women's Olympic Championship Tent Erection Team stared, hulking and dumbfounded.

There, before them all, the entire floor of the lagoon was paved in the brightest, most yellow, most pure GOLD TILES that anyone had ever beheld.

The sight gleamed so sharply, here in the strong moonlight, that everyone above had to squint to view it. If they had been seeing this during the daytime it would have been even more dazzling, and they would surely have needed the most powerful and protective sun-spectacles available.

"Mine," Bone gloated, his eyeballs glittering with the sight. "At last, mine, all mine! By Midas, it must be the size of a dozen soccer fields! Aaaaaaarrrrrrr!"

"Gold!" shouted Jim.

Bone stood, and turned on his heel. "You're right there, Jimbo! Gold the whole way through! The

Maharaja forced thousands of slaves to lay the floor with these golden beauties. Many of the slaves perished from the labour!"

"Barbaric," said Jim.

"So *that's* what went on up here," Doris said.

It suddenly occurred to Jocelyn what had blinded her, and what had sent the shafts of brilliant yellow light shooting up from the top of the crater. Maybe there had been some wind blowing across the water, or some disturbance within the lagoon, and the sun had speared down through a shallow part of the water, its rays bouncing and glinting off the golden floor below, and sending the bright, blinding light up through the shallows, spearing into the sky.

"According to Dr Schnitger," Bone continued ecstatically, "every single tile down there is twenty-four carat!"

"There must be fifty thousand of them!" Jim could barely believe that his eyes could take in the entire sight.

"Close, goody-boy, close." Bone took out his pocket-journal and flipped open the pages. "Schnitger counted 'em. He said there're fifty thousand, seven hundred and forty-two, exactly."

"Rark," Doris moaned. "It's giddy-making!"

"Quaaaaaooooo," Brenda snorted, feeling the heat inside the bulb rise further.

"The lagoon floor is revealed like this," Bone informed his captives, "only for one night every month, when the full moon affects the tide in the way you have just witnessed. It is, as Dr Schnitger wrote, a miracle of nature." He smiled rapturously. "And that which is left is a miracle of wealth!"

"But what are you going to do with it all?" Jim shouted. "How're you going to get it all out of there?"

"Oh, *I'm* not going to get it out. *I'm* not going to lift a precious manicured finger. No! What do you think I've brought the entire Turkish Women's Olympic Championship Tent Erection Team here for?"

Jim frowned. "I *thought* they looked familiar."

"The piastre's dropped," muttered Desdemona.

"Each of those powerful, massive women," Bone went on, "will have the pleasure of breaking up these tiles and lugging them down the path, once we have excavated the entire lagoon floor. No one will miss the women, you see. Like you, they are failures, although, *un*like you, they have their uses!"

"You're deranged, Bone! You're brutal, avaricious, selfish, parsimonious—"

"And you're *deady-bones*, Jim of Cairo, in a few very short minutes!"

"Crark!" Desdemona croaked.

Bone pulled out his fob-watch. "Desdemona, go and fetch the Twoctet. Tell them to bring the picks and mallets I have in my Travelling Trunkette. Their real work is about to commence."

"Aye, aye, my Captain."

"And don't dilly-dally. We only have five and a half hours before the moon causes the tide to turn. Then the water will rise once again from deep within Gunung

Dempo, and swamp the lagoon for another month." He shuddered. "These jungles are the last place I want to spend the next month in!"

"Nevermore, nevermore, nevermore!" She flew off to Fatimé Breeches and the other women.

"I shall be worth tens of billions," Bone leered, pocketing his fob-watch and wobbling excitedly.

"Jim!" screeched Doris, "I can feel something inside this thing. It's wet!"

"The indestructibilia juice!"

Brenda snorted wildly. "The smell," she thought. "The smell's arriving!"

Jocelyn and Jim smelled it too. It was pungent, vile, putrid.

"Let me help you," Jocelyn gasped, trying to prise a lobe-petal from Jim's neck. But her efforts were useless – she wasn't anywhere near strong enough to loosen them.

"Rark!" Doris wailed. "What're we going to do?"

She lifted her beak, and was about to screech again, to let rip with the loudest sound a macaw could make, when suddenly the golden floor of the lagoon gave a violent, ground-breaking shudder.

And a colossal rumble broke out from deep within Gunung Dempo.

AWAKENINGS

KAAAAAAAABBBBBBBBBBHHHHHHOOOOOOO
MMMMMMMMMMMMMM!

Fatimé Breeches stood defiantly before Bone, her powerful hands splayed across her hefty hips.

"The last thing I remember was something about 'fourchettes'," she snarled. "And you making promises to us!"

"Yes, you grubby little man," growled Kaynarca, standing behind her leader.

"What are we doing here?" blurted Dënise. "How did we get here from our headquarters in Istanbul?"

"This is not the lifestyle I chose," said Bernica, her granite features hardening.

All the colour had drained from Bone's face. "Desdemona!" he hissed. "Quick, give 'em some of that tea! Hurry!"

"Can't," replied the raven.

"What?" Bone's eyes were as wide as they had been when he had first glimpsed the floor of the lagoon.

"None left. It's all gone – them pills, I mean." She held the empty tube out in her talon.

He snatched it from her, and tipped it upside down. Nothing.

"But I told you to put only *two* pills into the samovar. There were over a dozen in this!"

"Two, a dozen, whatsa diff?"

"ANSWER OUR QUESTIONS, MAN!" Dënise was advancing threateningly, flexing her biceps and cracking her knuckles.

"Crark, I'm outta here!" Desdemona lifted her wings and shot off into the night sky, where she quickly became merely another smudge of shadow.

"You ungrateful wretch of a flying contraption!" Bone wailed. Then a thought occurred to him. "Wait a momentum ... if these women had an excessive amount of the Obsequious Pills, surely they should be obeying me even more?"

"TELL US: WHAT ARE WE DOING HERE?"

He flicked open his cigar-lighter and used the flame to read the tiny instructions on the side of the tube. "Warning: overuse of these Obsequious Pills will result in a return to a more strengthened state of disobedience!" The blood rushed from his fat cheeks. "Oh, dear, dear me ... just when I had everything within my—"

KAAAAAAAABBBBBBBBBBBHHHHHOOOOOO MMMMMMMMMMMMMM!

"Jim!" screeched Doris. "There it goes again!"

"What in the name of Ethel Merman?" stammered Cairo Jim.

"It's coming from down there," screamed Jocelyn. "From under the golden floor!"

"Quaaaaooooo!" Brenda snorted, wildly and warningly. *"The volcano! It's about to blow!"*

"Have mercy!" wailed Bone, as Dënise lifted him by his collar until his feet dangled off the ground.

"This volcano!" shouted Fatimé. "It's going to ERUPT!"

Suddenly the tiles in the floor of the lagoon heaved upwards, and began melting, fast becoming a sea of molten gold. A huge shaft of steam shot out from below, and the air filled with the smell of sulphur and burning rock.

With an ear-splitting CRASH a molten boulder spewed up from within the bowels of Gunung Dempo, blasting through the overhanging trees and setting them ferociously ablaze. The boulder hurtled into the sky and disappeared into the night, a burning flame of roundness.

"Quick," shouted Fatimé. "Get this man into that litter down there! We'll take him down the mountain, on that path out there. If we move quickly we can evade the lava!"

"Oh, thank you, thank you," grovelled Bone, as a wide torrent of bright orange and dark black lava began to pour up from the melted gold floor of the lagoon.

"Don't thank *me*," snarled Fatimé, as Dënise hoisted him over her wide shoulder and ran across the cracking courtyard. "We are going to settle our score with you as soon as we get clear of this inferno!"

"Yes," threatened Osmana, as Bone was hurled into the bamboo litter. "By the time we have finished with you, you will really know what a tent-peg feels like at the Olympic Games!"

"*Aaaaaaaaaaaaarrrrrrrrrrrr,*" came Bone's terrified wailings as the Turkish Women's Olympic Championship Tent Erection Team disappeared with him through the collapsing wall and down the pathway on the other side of Gunung Dempo.

"Wait!" hollered Jocelyn, but she was not heard above the roaring, sizzling tide of the lava, as it continued to spew forth below them.

"Scraaaarrrk!" screeched Doris. "The acid! The acid in the indestructibilia juice! I can feel it against my claws!"

Time swam about before Cairo Jim, as Jocelyn tried to pull the lobe-petals from Doris's neckfeathers. The macaw struggled, kicking her claws out of range of the indestructibilia juice, deep inside the flower, as best she could.

Jim struggled too, as did Brenda, but it was futile: the more they moved, the hotter it became inside the flower, and the tighter the lobe-petals closed about their necks.

The lava below was rising, getting higher and higher, swallowing up the lower ruins of the Palace of Srivijaya, toppling the unstable walls, engulfing the tree trunks, rapidly approaching the ledge where Jim, Doris, Brenda and Jocelyn were trapped...

The smell of sulphur was becoming stronger, sucking away the oxygen ...

...and then, in the beating of a heart, the flowers opened their petals. *Flooooommmmmp*! The indestructibilia juice stopped squirting around Doris's legs.

The temperature inside the cups dropped, and the lobe-petals returned to their usual opened position.

"Quaaaoooo!" Brenda dredged up more information from her encyclopaedic chambers: *"The only time that the* Rafflesia gargantua indestructibilia *does not issue the lethal acidic juice is when there is sulphuric activity in the vicinity. This renders the giant flowers dormant for six months, and harmless to any predators."*

Jim picked up the information, and relayed it quickly to the others. "I wouldn't give up reading for the world," he said when he had finished.

"Rark!" Doris fluttered up and out of the flower, stretching her wings as she darted about in the steamy, hot air. "That's better!"

"The crisis isn't over yet," announced Jocelyn. "Look, the lava! It's going to burn us in its path!"

Steadily the molten rock was creeping upwards, spewing over the outer walls of the Palace crater, rising towards the *Rafflesia* ledge. The stench of sulphur was dizzying.

"Rark! What now?"

As if a door had been thrown open, a thought dashed into Cairo Jim's head, and he blurted: "The flowers!"

"Quaaaooo!" Brenda nodded her head, agreeing quickly.

Jim clambered out of his flower, speaking breathlessly: "Hurry, no time to waste!" He got his machete from his knapsack (the Turkish women had dumped his knapsack conveniently beneath one of

the flowers) and started hacking away underneath the flower he'd been trapped in.

"What're you doing?" shouted Jocelyn.

A loud, encroaching spill of lava was hissing closer and closer.

"Trying to cut through the stem!" With frenzied thwacks he attacked the thick stem of the *Rafflesia*. "Remember what I said earlier? About how these flowers are seemingly indestructible? Well, if I can sever the stem, we're going to ride the lava flow, down the volcano, inside the *Rafflesia*!"

"Great thinking, Jim," screeched Doris, "but hurry!"

Jocelyn moved quickly as Jim continued hacking at the stem. "I'll get some vines – Brenda, come and give me the help of your strong snout. That way we can stay connected when we're in the *Rafflesias* – we can't all fit in the one, can we?"

"No," Jim grunted, smashing the machete wildly into the stem. Bits of the fleshy plant were flying off, but it was slow work. "Doris and I'll go in one, and you and Brenda in another. Try and get two good lengths of bamboo as well, Joss – we'll use those as steering poles, to help us stay upright, until they burn up in the lava!"

"Right!"

Frantically Jocelyn and Brenda ripped a long, sturdy length of vine from the remains of the wall behind them.

"There!" Jim shouted triumphantly as the stem was severed through. The flower above it teetered onto its side, resting on two of the lobe-petals. "Now for the next one!" He started attacking the second flower – the biggest on the ledge, and the one to take Brenda and Jocelyn.

Doris kept a worried eye on the lava. "Getting closer, closer, closer!"

Brenda found a clump of sturdy bamboo at the back of the *Rafflesia* cluster. Lowering her neck to the ground, she clamped her jaws around a stalk. With a sudden jerk of her neck, the stalk snapped off close to the ground.

Jocelyn took the bamboo from her, and the Wonder Camel repeated the action.

The perspiration was awash all over Jim as he kept hacking into the stem. Thwack after thwack after thwack ensued. The *Rafflesia* began to sway until finally, with a sluicing CRACK, the stem was cut completely.

"There! Now, quickly, *the lava will be burning our feet in a few seconds! Brenda, Joss, into the cup of this one!*"

Brenda lowered her back, lifted her hoofs, and climbed in. She flattened herself against the wall-like side of the flower's cup, and Jocelyn climbed in next to her.

"Quick, Jim!" Doris cried, as the lava crept right up to the heels of his boots.

In a flash, Jocelyn handed one of the bamboo poles to Jim, as well as one end of the vine.

"Quickly, Jim," she urged, "into the other flower!"

"Aarrrrrgh!" he felt the heat creep into his boots, and smelled the burning leather of his soles. With a grunt, he dived into the other *Rafflesia*, alongside Doris. She took the vine from him and clenched the end firmly in her beak.

"Stay calm everybody," he called. Now that he was

inside the cup of the flower, his boots cooled almost immediately.

The lava surged right up to the ledge, now, engulfing the *Rafflesia* group. It flowed across the flowers, and met the two *Rafflesia* in which Jim and Doris, Brenda and Jocelyn were sitting.

"Ooer," Jocelyn murmured, as her and Brenda's flower started to tilt. Quickly she passed her end of the vine to Brenda and leant out – being careful not to get too close to the lava – and used the bamboo pole to right the flower-vessel.

"That's it, Joss," called Jim, doing likewise with his pole.

Brenda and Doris held the vine taut between the two flowers.

Without warning, there was another almighty explosion from below.

KAAAAABBBBBBBBHHHHOOOOOMMMMM!

Tonnes of searing, molten rock flew into the sky.

The lava flow increased, spewing out from the crater with fresh anger, forcing the insides of the earth to the outside.

"We're moving faster!" screeched Doris.

The lava carried the two flowers up and over the walls of the Palace grounds, burning the rocks and the trees, the fronds and the vines all around. Like a great, searing tidal wave, it swept the two *Rafflesia* down the side of the volcano.

Everything around was being swamped in the on-

slaught of heat, but within the *Rafflesia* the temperature remained hot but bearable. The insulation was astonishing, thought Jim, as the flowers gushed downwards.

The flowers swivelled and turned, teetered and slid. All the time, Jim and Jocelyn used the poles to maintain the balance of the flowers.

The smell of sulphur and melting rock was overwhelming. Jocelyn tore her handkerchief in half, helped Brenda put one half into her nostrils, and then clamped the other half across her own nose.

Great, thick clouds of ash billowed all around.

The noise was almost deafening: a great wall of sound, like fiery bulldozers levelling everything in their path. The jungle crackled and crashed and hissed; the volcanoside groaned and crashed and crumbled.

KAAAAAAAAABBBBBBBBBBBHHHHHOOOOOO MMMMMMMMMMMMMM!

Down, down, down pushed the lava, flowing so fast that the night became a blur of orange. As if riding a wave on two rounded surfboards, down, down, down sped the four in their *Rafflesia* flowers.

Soon the bamboo poles had burnt so far up, they were short and useless, but by this time, they were unnecessary; the foursome were far from the crater, and surging towards the foothills.

As they approached the flatter regions, the lava gradually became cooler, and the speed of the flow slowed until it could be outwalked by those who wanted to continue their escape on foot, hoof and wing.

◎ ◎ ◎ ◎ ◎ ◎ **21** ◎ ◎ ◎ ◎ ◎ ◎

LOOKING BACK

"WELL," SAID JOCELYN, sitting by the wreckage of her Lockheed, far from the lava flowing down the other side of the volcano in the opposite direction, "I guess we found what Dr Schnitger was being so mysterious about."

"Quaaaaoo," snorted Brenda, between chomping the fresh green grass beneath her hoofs. *"And much more, besides…"*

"And much more besides, considering what might have happened to you, Joss!" Doris was perched on the Flight Attendant's knee and surveying the brilliantly fiery sky above Gunung Dempo.

Jim blinked, as did Jocelyn. "That's the first time you haven't called Joss by her full name," said the archaeologist-poet.

Doris nodded. "We've come a bit further than that, now."

Jocelyn stroked the ash from the macaw's crest.

"But not far enough for you to put ribbons in my plumage," squawked Doris.

Cairo Jim smiled – a weary smile, half-sad, half-relieved – at Jocelyn. "Yes, Joss, you must tell us what happened inside the volcano."

She pushed some curls from her forehead. Strange, mysterious things were often happening to her, especially whenever she travelled. "Believe me, as soon as I work it out, you three will be the first to know."

Jim sipped from his water bottle. "Strange, isn't it?" he said quietly.

Doris hopped across onto *his* knee. "What's strange, my friend?" she prowked, nestling herself against his torn and sooty shirt.

"How we all think we know so much, yet there are places like this that prove just the opposite."

Doris blinked, and turned her beak to gaze up at the dying volcano.

"Places that conceal the deepest mysteries, and so much forgotten knowledge."

"Quaaaaoooo," snorted Brenda the Wonder Camel, knowing all too well that there would be many such places ahead of them in the future.

Slowly, as the clouds of ash thinned, and the sulphur began to clear from the air and the lava surge slowed, and as the sun started to rise in the hazy distance, Brenda's thought spread into the heads of Jim, Doris and Jocelyn.

And, as one, they all tingled mightily at the prospect.

THE END